27 Days til Jubilee

SHAKIRA R. THOMPSON

LOVESTORY365

Author contact: shakira.r.thompson@gmail.com

Printed in the United States

First Printing, 2025

Contents

For Shakira at 50.

I marked this milestone by writing a birthday gift to myself.
And to all the Edens of the world, at any age and stage, who has
ever wondered if it's too late, if she's too much, or if she's missed her
moment: *Your Jubilee is Coming.*

Acknowledgements

We just hit ten books. That may not seem like much to some, but it feels monumental to me. After my last book, I questioned every writing ability I thought I had. I actually stopped writing. Part of that was due to professional obligations, but part of it was fear. It is hard to offer your heart and soul on the page and then watch people tear it apart like yesterday's newspaper.

Still, my spirit would not let this one go. Book number ten insisted on being born, and what better time than my fiftieth birthday. One morning, I woke up at two o'clock with a title placed fully in my heart. The message was clear. This had to be written now. I set everything else aside and began that very day.

For as long as I can remember, I have always wanted to write love stories. I am deeply grateful to be doing what lives in my heart. With that said, I must acknowledge my spiritual dream team. I have no doubts, The Holy Trinity walks with me whenever I write, and I will never apologize for what has been placed in my spirit.

I also acknowledge two of the brightest lights in my life. Charity and Keira, I know how you feel about writing season. For all the times I could not hear you or be fully present, I pray the Lord grants you a special blessing in exchange for allowing me the space to surrender to this calling. You are my greatest scripts, and I love you more than words could ever fully express.

I graciously acknowledge my sister friend who shared one interaction with me that seeded this storyline. May Jubilee catch you being your true, authentic self.

This book arrived quickly and with urgency. There was little time for anything beyond writing and publishing. I am deeply thankful for three women who graciously agreed to beta read and offer invaluable feedback that helped keep this story moving forward. Luician, Genine, and Coretta, under grace and in the most miraculous way, may Jubilee find you when you least expect it.

In every book I have written after my second, I acknowledge Shakira's Sweethearts, the U.S. G.I.R.L.S. book club. You taught me an important lesson with the last book. While it was not easy in the moment, it was deeply instructive, and I remain grateful for you all and the growth it required of me.

To my family and friends, those who have come and gone through the years and those who remain, thank you. I see the roles you play in my life, and I honor them.

And to everyone who will read this book, thank you. Truly. I mean that with my whole heart.

Thank you. Thank you. Thank you.

Prologue

The envelope arrived before dawn.

No messenger lingering at the door. Just the quiet click of a letter slot and the whisper of paper meeting marble.

The courier had been paid well for discretion. For timing and for understanding that some deliveries are less about logistics and more about legacy.

At fifty years old, Laurence and Milicent, also known as Millie McDonald, first laid eyes on her, all five pounds and nine ounces of fury and promise of her. They fell completely in love.

Infertility robbed them of having children of their own and stole the future they'd prayed for. Eden, however, became theirs in every way that mattered. She was christened to them as godparents, but she became their daughter, by devotion.

Eden's parents, John and Liora Williamson were business partners and good friends with the McDonalds. The Williamsons, having their own struggles with infertility, understood all too well. When Eden was born, she was like a miracle and gift to both families. She became "their girl."

Eden belonged to all of them. She is the firstborn. The miracle child. And then, later, her parents had more children.

The Williamsons and the McDonalds, bounded by not only friendship but a shared calling. The McDonalds were early investors and business mentors. Together, they built their political consulting firm; back when people still believed data could save nations and messaging could mend divides.

They weathered many victories, losses, and seasons of faith that asked more of them they sometimes wanted to give.

After Millie passed, Laurence lived on without her, carrying grief that mellowed him instead of hardening. With his ninetieth decade drawing to an end, his body entered a battle it could no longer win. Cancer slowed his steps and thinned his frame, but it never touched his devotion.

In the midst of his one-hundredth birthday approaching, a milestone he sensed he wouldn't reach, Laurence sat down to transcribe what he feared he wouldn't live long enough to say.

He entrusted the letter and its delivery to the law offices of Payne, Johnson and Davis, who handled it with the kind of reverence normally reserved for heirlooms.

Earlier in the year, Laurence passed peacefully after a brave battle with cancer, finally reuniting with his beloved Millie in eternity.

Yet even in death, he reached for Eden one last time. Words meant to guide and encourage her as she prepared for her upcoming birthday. He entrusted the letter's delivery to someone who could ensure it would reach her in time.

As unseen hands orchestrated its journey from law offices to courier routes to snowy streets, the letter landed atop a familiar pile on her marble entryway table.

Holiday cards, bills she'd avoided, glossy invitations to receptions she didn't want to attend, policy briefs she was too tired to read, December clutter at its finest. And somewhere within that mound, the thick, cream-colored envelope waited.

Day after day, the pile stared at her.

And day after day, she walked by it, choosing work, workouts, and anything else that kept her from the stress she didn't want to face.

And still it waited.

Her nephew had been in town for Thanksgiving, a rare overlap of schedules. Unbeknownst to her he intercepted the thick package from the courier and set it with the others.

For days, the envelope blended seamlessly with the usual clutter, waiting patiently for Eden's attention.

The click of Eden's heels crossing the threshold of hardwood floors and the clinking of her keys signaled her entrance.

"Thank you, Jesus, I'm finally home." Eden yelled out, her voice echoing and dissolving into stillness.

Everything turned on like clockwork. Her home came alive on cue. Lights rising, soft jazz filling the room, and temperatures adjusting, highlighted cues of a life ordered and controlled.

Setting about her evening routine, changing for her workout, slipping from the bold, ambitious lobbyist she was by day into the exercise enthusiast she was by night. Her fitness routine was more than exercise, it was therapy, a way to process the high-stakes, high-impact nature of her job.

It was her way of pushing back against a system that often felt too heavy to lift.

But tonight, something was different.

Was it a tug? A whisper? Or just a sense she was meant to pause? It was subtle enough to ignore but strong enough not to.

Before she could leave, a faint weight at the edge of the mail pile peeking out beneath a holiday card and caught her attention.

Dialing on her phone, calling her best friends, she said, "Hey girl, I'll meet you downstairs in a few minutes. I need to check out something really quick."

Hanging up, her steps faltered.

"Wait... what is this?" she whispered.

Stopping to pay closer attention, Eden's eyebrows drew together and then released.

A week of walking past it ended in single breath.

Weighty in nature, the envelope pressed softly in her hands, as if it carried more than just the elegant paper inside.

Faintly scented with lavender, Millie's favorite, with reverence, Eden peeled open the envelope to find the following letter:

"My dearest Eden, from the first day you came into our lives until my final days, I've had nothing but unconditional love for you. Millie and I loved you as if you were our very own. To watch you grow into the remarkable woman you are today has been one of my greatest joys.

You are about to embark upon a new chapter in your life. You are about to turn the same age Millie and I were when we first met you. That was a turning point in our lives, and I believe it will be for you as well.

I had to write this to you in case I wasn't here for your special birthday. As your godfather, I wanted you to know, I've seen you carry your burdens with grace beyond your own beliefs. But now, the time has come for you to release.

All that has been lost will be returned and all that is broken will be made whole. Prepare to receive restoration, joy, and love that's been waiting for you all along.

In the days to come, doors will begin to open for you, doors you thought were forever closed.

Trust the process, trust yourself, and trust the One who's never left your side.

God has not forgotten you. Your Jubilee is coming.

Your Loving Godfather,

Laurence McDonald.

Feeling a shiver run down her spine, the words penned by Laurence pricked her.

The words blurred as tears gathered. Her throat tightened. Tremors ran through her fingers.

Bringing her shaky hands to her face to wipe her tears, Eden tried processing the moment. Laurence's words were written through earthly proxy but somehow his presence seemed to have reached through time and space.

The letter wasn't a goodbye; it was prophetic.

Waves of emotions cracked open inside her, raw and unexpected. Pressing a hand to her mouth, a soft whimper escaped, one too tender to stop.

He spoke directly to parts of her she'd never shared with anyone. Yet hope began to bloom where doubt resided for far too long.

Amara Adams, Eden's best friend, tired of waiting downstairs, constantly dialed her phone.

Her phone vibrated. Again. And again.

Retreating inward, Eden couldn't answer the phone.

How could she?

Divine inclinations were staring at her in the face, from the grave.

She couldn't leave the letter. She stayed rooted, absorbing every word. Every intent. Every promise.

Moments later, using her spare key, Amara stepped inside.

"Really?" Eden said wiping her face.

"Ma'am; I thought you said you were going to be down in a few minutes. What are you in here doing?"

With difficulty forming responses, Eden handed the letter to Amara, leaning her back against the wall, still processing.

Amara read it once, then whistled low. "Well. Okay then. God Daddy Laurence, I see what you're doing here. Girl, it looks like you're about to walk into your everything season."

"My everything season?" Eden asked, voice small and awed.

"Yes girl, your everything season," Amara said, dropping the letter to her side and pointing. "Your man, your money, your miracles, all of it, your everything! At once."

Trying to laugh at her friend, Eden was emotionally confused. Grief and hope collided in her chest, causing her to sob.

"This can't be real life."

"Says who? The woman who's been holding her breath for two years waiting for the other shoe to drop."

Eden's throat tightened.

"Listen," Amara said. "I don't know what's coming. But Laurence knew you. And he wouldn't have written this if it wasn't true."

Laurence's words were now a guiding light, an invitation. A gentle nudge into a chapter she'd been too tired, too wounded, and too busy to ask God for anymore.

His words were invisible, yet palpable.

The first ripples of Eden's Jubilee were starting to flow but was she ready to embrace it?

Chapter 1

P ale gold light switched on from the night's shadows, making a slow climb over the city's skyline, pushing night into the corners of Eden's bedroom.

Eden woke to the alarm she'd set the night before, then the backup alarm seven minutes later, then the third alarm that was less a precaution than a moral failing.

She hadn't slept well, not the deep restorative sleep she usually fought for. She drifted, waking in fragments, hearing Laurence's voice echo between dreams.

"I've seen you carry your burdens with grace...."

Taken a glance at her phone for the time, she forced herself upright, *"I should really get up and get ready for work."*

Right now, work was the only anchor she had, the routine, the structure. The familiar rhythm of being competent and in control.

Any other day, Eden was up and ready, yet now, every routine more seemed...heightened.

The sunlight slanting across the floorboards looked brighter.

When she finally stood, the floor was cold enough to make her reconsider her entire life.

Is this, she thought, what fifty looks like? *A woman negotiating with cold hardwood.*

Her morning devotional, which she usually read half-distracted while multitasking, felt startlingly direct, like scripture leaned across the table and whispered to her.

She moved through her morning routine with the efficiency of someone who optimized joy right out of the process. Shower: eight minutes. Skincare: four. Matcha: ceremonial grade, because if she was going to drink grass clippings, they'd better be expensive grass clippings.

"Jubilee," she said under her breath, testing the weight of the word.

Somehow, it didn't feel distant.

The reflection staring back at her wasn't the version she'd grown accustomed to.

Her eyes were softer. More open. More...expectant.

Finishing her morning matcha concoction, she reviewed her schedule for the day.

A meeting with Donovan Rivera was scheduled for mid-morning.

His name alone stirred a spark of curiosity she couldn't explain.

Two years ago, they met for business. Brief and pointed, Eden focused on the work at hand. Now the memory of that meeting felt distant, almost like someone else's life.

Chimes from her phone brought her back to her actual life. Amara was checking in, of course.

"Morning, girl. You good?" Amara's voice was all joking, carrying a smile Eden could hear through the line.

Allowing herself a small laugh, Eden said, "I'm awake, I promise."

"Uh-huh," Amara teased. "Sure. You don't really sound awake. You sound like someone who's just been handed the keys to the kingdom."

Shaking her head, Eden smiled saying, "Something like that," leaving the explanation at that.

"Well, you were a little topsy-turvy last night. So, I was just calling to check on you. I know you have a busy day but you're calling me on your lunch break.

"Yes ma'am."

"You better," Amara said before hanging up.

Perusing her closet, Eden's fingers swiped every item hanging trying to decide what to wear.

When her fingers paused, she heard in her spirit, "*This one.*"

Here fingers landed on a rich forest green dress she'd never worn, more sophisticated and feminine than her normal navy-blue suits.

Confidence wasn't new to Eden; she carried it like armor. Today however, it felt less like protection and more like an expression.

Stepping into the elevator, Eden held onto her things preparing for the long ride down.

Most days, with each passing floor number that glowed, Eden often wondered why she chose to live so high up in the sky.

Today, it felt like the elevator was a speed rail, sinking through the building as if it was burrowing into earth.

On the short walk to her firm, the December air bit at her cheeks, brisk but invigorating. Her breath puffed out in clouds as if the cold was trying to remind her, she was fully here, fully alive.

Inside the lobby, warm air and the scent of pine from the holiday display wrapped around her life a soft welcome.

Stepping off the elevator onto her floor, she was met with a flurry of activity.

"Whoa, you look fabulous today." One colleague said walking by.

"Oh, so only today? I don't look fabulous every day?" Eden replied smiling and with grace making the admiration stick.

"Wow," another said. "Okay, Miss Eden, I see you!"

Keeping her focus on the way to her office, the compliments continued to pour in from everyone who caught a glimpse.

"Hot date tonight?" Her work bestie asked peeking in to say good morning.

"*Why is everybody complimenting...today? I don't know what they're talking about, I look fabulous every day!*" She thought rummaging through stacked notes and schedules on her desk.

Her hair and makeup were the same. But apparently a shift had taken place because people were seeing her differently.

Or maybe, she was seeing herself.

In her office, her calendar lit up with reminders. Meetings stacked from morning to evening. And right in the middle:

Meeting with Donovan Rivera — 10:30 a.m.

The presentation slide deck for Donovan Rivera's meeting popped up on her computer as an email and a reminder. Eden was grateful, weeks before, she'd paired her assistant, Katy with his executive administrator, Marcel.

Marcel Rogers, Donovan's detail-obsessed right-hand man who treated logistics like a spiritual practice made sure everything for the meeting would run smoothly.

Reviewing the agenda, she thought, "*Why does this man's name sound familiar? Have we met before? I don't know, I guess we'll find out in a few minute*s."

Men in her line of work rarely lingered in memory unless they were exceptionally rude or exception in other ways.

A phone call from Thomas Richards, the President of her company delayed Eden to the meeting.

"Great, what now?" She exclaimed before answering.

The call, taking longer than she expected, officially made her late.

Grabbing her portfolio, she smoothed her dress, and hurried towards the boardroom, with her almost empty cup of an iced matcha latte.

Stepping into the boardroom triggered every head to turn in her direction. There was however, only one pair of eyes caught and held hers.

Donovan stood as she entered.

It'd been two years since he last saw her. In that time, she'd quietly been rebuilding herself. Physically she'd made changes, such as cutting her hair short and whew, the Pilates, yes, they were paying off in all of the right places.

"Good morning, everyone," she said composed. "My apologies for the delay." Eden said greeting everyone around the table.

"Hi Eden, not sure if you remember me but it's good to see you again."

Vaguely but not entirely. She couldn't place him. Too much life happened between then and now. There'd been too many fires to put out. The look on her face gave him the answer he was looking for.

Lifting his hands in surrender, he said, "Of course you don't remember me and my ugly face."

Someone stifled their laughter.

Which is funny because the man looks like a Renaissance painting that should probably pay its own taxes.

Introductions from both teams began as they were seated across from each other at the long boardroom table.

Donovan starts talking.

Fully focused and collected, Eden is taking notes.

Slipping into policy mode, Donovan is articulating each point with evidence. Every recommendation has rationale.

He keeps talking.

And keeps talking.

And continues to keep talking.

The morning's strategy session included Donovan reviewing policy drafts with meticulous precision. As a seasoned public policy attorney, legislative complexities were what he lived for.

Donovan continues talking until suddenly, looking directly at Eden, he says, "I feel like I'm talking too much. I guess that's why I'm probably still single."

Pens stop moving.

Every head around the table shifts towards Eden, who doesn't look up but feels the room tilt.

Donovan Rivera, the kind of man people call when things are complicated. Having spent his career assisting leaders navigate legislative, corporate, and governmental storms, he's sharp.

However, his awkward overshare was far from sharp. It wasn't smooth but it was sincere.

The board room heard a man fumbling.

Eden experienced something different, curiosity.

Before anything else could unfold, her meeting timer chimed.

Saved by the bell.

"I apologize but I must leave for another meeting. I'm sure my team will update me on everything. Have a great day everyone."

Stepping into the hallway, Eden let out a breath she didn't realize she'd been holding.

"What on earth was that? Was that his attempt at a joke? A confession? Was he trying to be charming?" Eden thought smiling.

Her questions hung around in the air, warm and unsettled, as she walked away to her next meeting.

Chapter 2

"You sound tired," Liora said without a greeting. "Are not sleeping again?"

"Well, I laid horizontally, that should count for something, right?"

"That means you didn't sleep," her mother corrected. "You've got too much on that mind of yours. Have you eaten breakfast?"

"I've had my matcha?"

"So...no."

"Mama, I'm fine. Work is just...a lot."

Eden wasn't ready to share Laurence's letter with her parents.

"Well, good. I'm calling to remind you we're getting together later this month. Your daddy and I want to do something for what would have been Laurence's hundredth. It won't be anything big, but you know how we feel."

"Yes Mama, I know."

"And we need to know what you're doing for your birthday too," her mother added gently. "Have you decided on anything?"

"No Mama, I haven't but as soon as I do, I'll be sure to let you know."

"Well, don't wait too long. You know it'll be here before you know it."

"Yeah, I know. It feels like it's coming fast."

"Baby, time is running quicker than people these days. But I know you're busy so don't let me keep you. Call me later and tell me what 'a lot' mean. And remember to breathe today."

"I will Mama."

"And eat some actual food."

"Yes ma'am, I'm working on that."

"Love you, baby."

"Love you too Mama."

Liora hung up first, as she always did.

Staring at her phone, one hundred years. Laurence used to joke about turning a hundred, as if he'd been training for the Centurion Olympics or something.

Lunchtime was creeping up, but Eden was deep into the project that brought Donovan presented on earlier, a large-scale community revitalization initiative. Her firm was tapped to lead the strategic development, but they needed an expert in multi-market operational expansion.

Therein lies Donovan.

His expertise would steer compliance, policy planning, and structural integrity.

Scribbling notes across her digital planner, she wrote:

· *Long-term scalability*
· *Regulatory implications*
· *Stakeholder mapping*

·   *Reach out to Donovan for his take on the projection inconsistencies.*

Peeking her head in Eden's office, Katy said, "Hey, got a sec?"

"For you I do, come in."

Holding a folder and wearing a grin that said, *"I know something,"* Katy pushed right in and sat in front of Eden's desk.

"Boy, do I have some tea for you!"

"I trust everything went well with the rest of the meeting after I left?"

"Yes, but we can talk about that later."

"I'd really like to hear how the rest of the meeting went."

Flapping her hands, Katy said, "Okay, okay I have two things. After you left Donovan said he appreciated how you laid out the stakeholder model."

"Good. That'll help the next phase move faster."

"Okay, now can I tell you the interesting part?"

"Sure, what is this tea you have for me?"

Leaning in like they were about to trade national secrets, Katy shared, "Marcel said, and I quote, you know Donovan looked her up two years ago. Before they ever met."

Baffled, Eden said, "Looked me up how?"

"My man did a whole social media deep dive, you know, a professional one. He checked out your background. Where you went to school. What your firm specializes in. Supposedly, he was 'curious about alignment.'"

Eden's head flinched back slightly, "Alignment?"

"Yeah, apparently when your name was mentioned in some cross-regional project, he did his research on your girl."

"Alignment huh?"

"Even I don't use words like that unless I'm trying to flirt professionally."

"Nah, he was just doing his job."

"Sure," Katy said, drawing out the word like she didn't believe her at all. "And I go to the gym for the free air conditioning. Because what was that why I'm single comment about?"

At this point, Eden could not stop laughing. Because what was that all about?

Right on schedule, Eden's phone lit up with Amara calling.

"Oh my goodness, I skipped lunch and forgot to call her. Katy, let me take this call."

"Sure thing, tell Amara I said hi."

"You said to call on my lunch break. I haven't gone to lunch yet."

"Yes, I know. I talked to your mom. So, I figured I'd call you and invite you to dinner tonight. My treat. This way, we'll both know you ate something today."

"But why are you treating?"

"Because friendship is my ministry. I'm just a good friend like that. And because I'm nosey. I need to know in full details how did the meeting with Mr. Tall-Dark-and Market-Expansion go?"

"It was...fine."

"Fine?" Amara scoffed. "The way you said fine doesn't sound fine."

"Amara, it was a good meeting. Productive. Clear. Efficient. Fine."

"Uh-huh. And did he smile at you the way he smiles in his headshots?"

"Umm, I don't know how he smiles in his headshots."

"Oh, I do," Amara said. "I investigated. Thoroughly. You know how I cyber-sleuth."

"Oh my goodness, you are too much." Eden said laughing.

"Indeed I am. Just call me team too much and don't think I forgot. You will meet me at seven o'clock tonight. Dinner. Drinks. A full vibe. And wear something that reminds the world you are fearfully and wonderfully made."

"Amara..."

"Don't argue with me. I'll see you later."

"How can I argue with you; I'll see you later."

***

The *Garden and Grain* was warm, cozy, and buried under soft lights. Exposed beams and velvet seating, with a DJ over in the corner playing the soundtrack of their youth.

The entire atmosphere was a whole vibe.

Spotting Eden walking in, Amara gasped dramatically, "Girl, you look like someone prayed Psalms 23 over you this morning."

"Stop it." Eden said blushing.

"No, I mean it. Did you moisturize with the Holy Spirit or something because Girl, you are glowing."

Seated in a nice section where they could people watch and enjoy the music; they started the night with appetizers and drinks.

Catching up on the day from their lunch conversation, Amara was updating Eden on one of her latest projects.

Pausing mid-sentence, she said, "Okay so, I'm so serious right now but don't look. You are catching some real attention in here tonight."

Eden didn't look. "Amara, please. I'm sure you're exaggerating."

"Seriously, I'm not. Table twelve just did a double take. You know the kind men do when they realize they've been living wrong. Yep, that just happened."

Sipping on her favorite drink, an old-fashioned, one with an orange peel, not a cherry, Eden said, "I've known you long enough to know you're being funny right now."

"I promise you I'm not. And now table eight is looking. Um, did you open up some kind of portal or something?"

Eden laughed so hard the server passing by smiled at her.

But Amara wasn't done. "Okay so now table four. Table four is fine fine. Beard, sport coat, he looks like he reads hardback books for fun and listens to podcasts about growth."

Amara reached for her phone. "Here, let's take a selfie so I can send it to Grant. He can see the dinner he's sponsoring."

"Woman, you are insane. He looks like he listens to podcasts about growth? How do you come up with this stuff? That is hilarious."

Amara snapped the picture.

Shaking her finger in the air, Amara said, "But I'm not insane because Mr. Hardback Books is walking over here right now."

For the first time, Eden realized Amara wasn't joking around.

"Wait, What? No. Why?"

"Uh, because you look like God said, 'Let there be light' and meant you, that's why."

"Amara, I seriously can not with you." Before Eden could continue, a deep voice said, "Excuse me ladies."

Tentative smiles that grew as they both looked up greeted the guy.

He was spectacular, looking like God created him on a day when He was feeling artistic. He was definitely confident but not in a way that took up all the air in the room.

"Excuse me," he said voice smooth. "I hope I'm not interrupting. Would you mind if I joined you for a minute?"

Shifting over to make room, he sat down and said, "I'm about to leave but I wanted to let you know your dinner tonight is on me. I took care of it," nodding towards their table. "I didn't want to be rude and send something without saying hello."

Turning into the human embodiment of well praise God, Amara started motioning gratitude.

Blinking, Eden said, "You...what? Why?"

Smiling gently, he looked at Eden. Only Eden. "Because of you. You have a presence that's hard to miss and a presence I wanted to meet."

Swallowing hard with a quickening heartbeat she said, "Well, that's very kind of you. Thank you."

Extending a business card he shared, "My name is Christopher. Christopher Wells and you are?"

In handing her his card and her receiving it, their fingers brushed and a small electrical current sparked between the two.

"Hi, I'm Eden."

"Hi, I'm Amara."

Looking directly at Eden, Christopher said, "If you'd ever like to grab coffee, I'd love that."

"I....might."

Smiling, slow and deliberate, like he already knew she would, he said, "Then I hope you do. It was nice meeting you both. Enjoy the rest of your evening. Good night."

As soon as he was out of earshot of them, Amara grabbed the table and said, "GIRL!"

Hiding behind her hands, Eden said, "What just happened?"

"I don't know, you tell me," Amara said looking over the menu to order my food. "Go ahead and create a contact in your phone and lock him in NOW!"

Picking up her phone to secure Christopher's contact information, Eden noticed an email notification.

From: Donovan Rivera

Subject: Today's Meeting

Inhaling slowly, she clicked.

Eden,

Thank you for your insight and leadership during today's meeting. I appreciate the clarity you brought to the stakeholder model. If you're open to it, I'd like to continue the discussion on scalability later this week.

~ Donovan

Chapter 3

Waking up the way people do when their minds start running before their eyes open, Eden was half-annoyed, half-surrendered, all tangled up in her sheets.

Turning over, reaching blindly for her phone, Eden groaned, her mind was already running a marathon.

Christopher's boldness flashed first. That smile of his. Good Lord, it hit her like warm cinnamon in a cold kitchen.

Donovan's email elbowed its way into her mental collage... *Thank you for your insight and leadership during today's meeting.* These words made her think he absolutely typed with his back straight and his moral compass polished.

Amara's voice barreled next, loud enough pushing Donovan's email out of the way. Her voice sounding as vivid as if she were standing there in the room. "*He looks like he reads hardback books for fun and listens to podcasts about growth,*" and "*Mr. Tall-Dark-and-Market-Expansion,*" took up top real estate in her mind.

Eden groaned into her pillow.

Her eyes drifted to the letter on the nightstand, Laurence's letter.

Her mother's voice floated behind it, gentle and earnest: "*Remember, we want to do something small for what would have been Laurence's hundredth...*"

Her birthday. His would-have-been birthday. The holidays. The deadlines. It all pressed against her temples like a tight winter headband.

Winter's bite snipped at Eden's cheeks as she scurried to her office. Snow crunched under her black and gold heeled boots down the sidewalk, as she dodged a patch of ice, she wasn't prepared to sacrifice her dignity to.

Tugging the wool scarf around her neck tighter, she fumbled with the keycard, delaying her entrance into the building. Because naturally, a small struggle must accompany every winter morning.

Inside, the lobby's warmth hit first.

By the time she reached her office, her mind felt clearer; either from the cold or because her brain decided to take a temporary union break.

Sitting down, she slid into her chair and clicked her inbox open.

There it was again.

Donovan's email.

Still polite. Still earnest. Still...Donovan.

She was about to reread it when a new email pinged.

> **From**: Metropolitan Community Equity Alliance
>
> **Subject**: A Review of Public Access to Community Spaces

"Oh no," she whispered. "Not today."

She opened it.

The organization wanted her to lead a citywide review of underinvestment in public-access anchors; libraries, community centers, churches, and parks. Additionally, they requested she present the findings to the board *next week*. Maps. Data. Disparities. Politics. Pressure.

"Perfect," she muttered, kicking her chair back an inch. "Just perfect. I love this journey for me."

Tasting the bitter metal taste of fear or was it responsibility, either way, she inhaled, then exhaled.

Reaching into her drawer for pens, her fingers brushed something unfamiliar. A creamy, elegant envelope. One that was not there yesterday.

Staring at it, she said, "Oh, no. Not again." Pressing her palm to her forehead, "If this is another letter from Laurence from the great beyond, I'm out. I will simply walk into the snow and let the Lord decide my fate."

Touching the smooth surface of the envelope that bore her name with her fingertips, she had a decision to make.

Would she dare to open it?

Her phone buzzed with the name **Amara** glowing across the top.

"Hello there Gorgeous!" Amara's voice erupted, impossibly cheerful. "Any new fine men buy you breakfast yet?"

Looking at the envelope like it might detonate, Eden said, "Nope. I think that was just an isolated incident. Plus, I can't even think about eating breakfast because I literally have bigger fish to fry."

"What do you mean by that? What kind of fish? Salmon? Catfish? Tuna?" Amara asked.

"Does opening an urgent policy assignment while finding another mysterious note count as bigger fish to you?" Eden asked.

"Oh, it counts. It definitely counts. What does the note say?"

"I don't know because I haven't opened it yet. I found it right before you called. How did this even get here, Amara? Things don't just...materialize in drawers."

"Okay, I see it was meant for me to call you so WE could open the note together. I'm here with you Girl. Go ahead and open it. I'm curious to know what's inside."

Attempting to prolong opening the note, Eden said, "You know what? When does Grant get home? Because your boredom is dangerous."

As an empty-nester Amara was somewhat bored but she was also working on other projects trying to figure out the next phase of her life. She was genuinely invested in her friend's life. She just processed life through humor.

"Eden, please stop trying to come for me. You're only deflecting because you're scared. But I'm here with you Girl."

"When does your husband come home?" Eden repeated.

"Grant's out of town until Thursday. I miss him, but it means I get to borrow his credit card guilt-free. Until then, you better get all the Amara you can stand right now."

Eden laughed and slid her finger under the flap and ripped open the envelope.

Inside, was a white card, with simple handwriting, and four words:
Be Kind to Yourself Today.

Eden's fingers lingered on the note card, tracing each word as if to try and memorize them.

Caught somewhere between disbelief and delight, she laughed as Amara squealed.

"I knew it!"

"You knew what?"

"That somebody was going to buying you breakfast this morning. Now, I may have been off slightly but someone is definitely feeding you today. It's giving a divine romantic comedy."

"Amara, please."

"You know what? It might be Christopher. Maybe he knows a guy who knows a guy with keys to your office."

"Why would you say that? That doesn't help me and that would be kind of creepy."

"You're right, he doesn't know where you work. I just got a little carried away and excited. Anyway, speaking of Christopher, have you called that fine man yet?"

"Christopher? No, I .... haven't."

"What? And why not? This man practically moonwalked into your life and you're just what...dilly-dallying like it's a three-day weekend?"

"I'm not dilly-dallying Amara. I'm ...strategizing. Eden said smirking.

"Well, strategically hang up the phone with me and call him now!"

"Now?!"

"Right now! Before I drive over there and dial the number myself."

"I promise it's not that serious."

"Eden. Call. The. Man."

"How has me calling Christopher become an item on your to-do list?" Eden said laughing.

"Eden, call the man and text me a full report. I need clarity by close of business. Bye!"

Following Amara's instructions, she scrolled through her contacts to find Christopher's information before she backed herself out from calling.

Answering on the first ring.

"Good morning."

Warm. Smooth. The kind of voice that'll make your spine say thank you.

"Christopher?"

"Yes, this is Christopher. Who's this?"

"Hi, this is Eden. We met last night. I...uh...I wanted to thank you again for dinner. Amara and I had a wonderful time."

"Mission accomplished."

Eden and Christopher slipped into an easy rhythm of conversation. Sharing little stories, shared jokes with tiny details exchanged like early Christmas gifts. Their camaraderie made Eden's office feel like a snow globe was shaken just for them.

Eden felt herself smiling more than she had all morning.

"So, how's your workday going so far?" Christopher asked with a careful voice.

"Um, let me see. Imagine if Christmas came early and left a mountain of work under the tree for me. Yeah, that's today."

"Ah, I see. Well, take one bite of the elephant at a time. And be kind to yourself in the process."

Her eyes flicked to the note card.

"*Is he serious right now? Oh my, is Amara right? Did he send me this note? That's impossible. There's no way.*" Eden thought.

Captured by her thoughts, Eden got quiet on the phone.

"Eden?" he asked. Do you disappear often or is that reserved for special occasions?"

"Oh yes, I apologize. I'm here. What were you saying?"

"I asked if you would you like to grab coffee? Maybe this Saturday?"

Before her overthinking cap could hijack her, she said, "Yes, I'd love to."

"Saturday it is. Is this a good number to contact you on?" Christopher asked.

"Yes, you can contact me here."

"Perfect. I'll reach out to you later with more details. Take care."

Hanging up the phone, Eden picked up the note card and read it aloud, "Be Kind to Yourself Today."

She slid the card carefully into her planner, the one she reserved for new ideas, big dreams, and God-sized projects.

Clicking open the equity foundation email, she typed:

I would be honored to support this initiative. However, a presentation next week won't allow for meaningful work. I can have my assistant coordinate a time to meet with your team at the start of the new year to set a realistic and strategic timeline.

Happy Holidays.

Chapter 4

The first workweek in December was almost complete. Friday arrived and the building had fully surrendered to Christmas. Overnight, the decorators transformed the building into a Winter Wonderland. Silver garland snaked along the railings, twinkling lights climbed columns, and when the sliding doors open, the whole lobby shimmered like it was dusted with fresh Christmas magic.

Entering the building, Eden paused for a second, allowing the holiday glamour to wash over her. Only one more day until her coffee date with Christopher and she was excited.

They'd been talking every day since the first call, and the anticipation was building.

"Good morning, Eden," Katy said, her voice bright as a string of fairy lights. Perched at her workstation, laptop half-open, she was waiting for Eden to arrive for the day.

"Morning," Eden said, sliding her gloves off and offering a small smile before continuing toward her office.

Within seconds, Katy appeared in Eden's doorway like sunshine in boots, holding a mug that read: *Be Nice to Me, I'm Magic.*

Walking straight in, she settled herself on the edge of Eden's desk like she paid rent there.

"Hey superstar, you good?"

"Yeah, why do you ask?"

"Oh, only because..." Katy squinting playfully. "You're glowing. And no, it's not the office heater. You've got something going on."

Eden's cheeks warmed as soon as Katy closed in on her. She smoothed an imaginary crease from her sleeve, trying to sound casual, she said, "Well...I mean."

Her voice bobbled like it hit a speed bump. "I might have a little something going on. Actually, I'm meeting someone for coffee tomorrow."

Nearly slipping off Eden's desk, Katy's eyes widened, you would think Eden told her she'd been cast as Beyonce's understudy.

"A coffee date? With who? Do I know him?"

"His name is Christopher. Amara and I met him at dinner the other night at *The Garden and Grain.*"

"Oh yeah, I've heard that place is really nice. I've been meaning to check it out, I just haven't gotten by there yet." Katy shared.

"Yes, it's very nice. We had a blast!"

Tapping her lip thoughtfully, she said, "Maybe that's where Marcel and I will go this weekend."

Katy dropped the announcement like she was tossing confetti at a parade, waiting to see if Eden caught the reference.

Stopping mid-stride, Eden said, "You and Marcel? Am I missing something here?"

Katy shrugged, all innocence. "Uh, he likes me and I think I like him too. But trust, we're keeping things professional where it matters.

Nothing to worry about." Leaning in she said, "But back to *you*. Tell me more about Christopher. Show me a picture. I know you've looked him up online."

"No, I haven't looked him up, but I do have a picture."

Looking at his picture, Katy shouted, "Oh he is fine! Yes, please tell me more about this coffee date."

"Calm down. It's just coffee."

"Uh-huh," Katy said crossing her legs, with her eyebrows arched like she was reading footnotes on Eden's heart. "Could Christopher be Birthday-Bae? I mean because what are we doing for your 50th? You've been dodging that question like it owes you money or something."

Eden opened her mouth, then closed it. "I...I still don't know yet."

With everything going on Eden felt like her birthday loomed like a test she hadn't studied for.

Softening, Katy tilted her head, "Um, that's honest. We can work with honest. Turning 50 is nothing to dismiss, you're about to be half a hundred. We have to celebrate."

"Did you have to bring up the half of a hundred?" Eden said with a sneer.

"Did I lie though," Katy said shrugging her shoulders like a balancing scale. "But seriously, it's an important time. It's your personal Jubilee year."

"*Here we go with that word again*," Eden thought to herself.

Pointing in the direction next to Eden, Katy asked, "What is all *this*?"

Drawing Eden's attention to the side table near her desk, a Dove chocolate bar sat wrapped in gold foil, a small note card taped neatly to the top.

"Here we go again. Did you see who put this in here?" Eden asked picking up the gift.

Katy leaned back like she had nothing to hide, though her hands gripped her mug tighter.

"I wish I could answer that," she said.

Becoming accustomed to opening mysterious notes, Eden slowly peeled the card free. It read:

This is your invitation to renounce old agreements. Today, break up with every belief keeping you small. Like the candy bar reflects, release them like doves. Because the truth is, you're not behind. You haven't missed your chance. You don't have to do everything alone.

Eden pressed her fingertips to her lips, her breath catching. She blinked hard, but the words didn't fade.

The note felt like someone had read her diary at 2 a.m. and wrote her a survival plan.

"Wow," Katy whispered. "That's pretty powerful Eden. So, Dove bar today, Christopher tomorrow...I'm telling you, he might be Birthday-Bae after all."

Eden sighed and shrugged, shoulders loosening. "I keep saying this—things don't just materialize out of nowhere. How is this stuff getting in here?"

Repeating her well-rehearsed response, Katy said, "I wish I could answer that for you."

Hopping off Eden's desk she said, "Maybe you should treat this like an adventure or a little scavenger hunt of sorts. Let it be fun. I say, eat your chocolate bar and do whatever the little note says. Let it work on you. You deserve this. This could be your Christmas miracle."

Eden believed in miracles, but she'd never really experienced the ones like in the Bible, the God can move mountains kind. She wasn't sure miracles were really for her.

But miracles, apparently, were ready for her.

Opening the door to leave Eden's office, Donovan walked past. His coat draped elegantly over one arm, his attention focused on his phone, until he glanced up and noticed them. Offering a polite nod, he continued down the hallway, leaving the subtle aroma of his cologne lingering like punctuation.

Just enough to keep him noticeable.

Just enough to make her sit a little straighter.

Katy, following Eden's gaze said, "Okay Mr. Donovan looking a distraction.

"Katy – "

"What? I'm simply observing," raising her mug, she said, "And supporting. We're going to get Birthday-Bae one way or another.

"I can't with you Katy. But you have to go. I have a meeting. We'll catch up later."

Chapter 5

"This place loves a Friday night. It's crowded in here."

Music pulsed out the doorway and the crowd inside hummed with every reason people left their house during the holidays.

Marcel, holding the door open for Katy, let her pass ahead of him like the Southern gentleman he was raised to be.

Stepping into a swirl of candlelight, amber-toned bulbs and a playlist, one cinnamon stick short of a Christmas cocktail, The Garden and Grain was alive, giving seasonal overflow.

Walking towards the hostess desk for their reservations, Katy snapped her fingers along with the beat, with her hips swaying ever so slightly.

"Oh, I get it now," she said. "If the food is even half as good as this music, I might end up becoming a member. But Eden raved about this place and I trust her."

"Speaking of tasting good," Marcel said with a strong sense of playfulness, leaning down, "You look delicious."

Sliding him a frisky, don't start nothing you can't finish smile, she said, "So you're planning to order something off menu tonight, huh?"

"Right this way," the hostess beckoned. Ushering them towards their booth, weaving them through hundreds of conversations, bursts of laughter, clinking glasses, and the faint scent of rosemary drifting from the kitchen.

Sliding into their own velvet booth under a hanging lantern. Marcel took another approving look around. He liked the place Katy picked out. Their section was cozy, intimate, and dim enough to inspire confessions.

A server approached bearing gifts, the kind of breadbasket that would cause angels to peek over clouds. Warm, fragrant, and fresh enough to steam when torn open. Little curls of homemade butter sat beside it like tiny promises.

Inhaling dramatically, Katy said, "Now this is how you deliver bread, very detailed. And details matter tonight, my friend."

"Oh?" Marcel said leaning in, his eyes warmed with a hint of mischief. "And which details are we talking about... friend?"

"The ones about Eden."

Coughing into his bread. "Eden? Katy, are we working tonight or are we on a date?

"Both?"

"What are you up to Katy? Should I brace myself? This feels like are we about to enter into holiday shenanigans territory?"

"Guilty as charged," Katy admitted, shrugging her shoulders, then tapping his hand lightly. "I want to tell you something. It may sound crazy, but I trust you."

Marcel straightened, giving her his full attention. His version of intimacy was subtle but unmistakable.

"Alright. I'm listening, enlighten me."

Taking a small breath, Katy explained.

"Ever since you told me Donovan looked Eden up two years ago, something's been brewing in my spirit. Then we had that meeting, and he dropped that very awkward 'still single' comment, straight at Eden. I swear it felt like the man's soul tripped out of his body."

Marcel laughed so hard the couple in the next booth glanced over smiling. "I've worked with Donovan for six years and I've never heard him slip like that."

"So," Katy continued, "you see it too?"

"I mean...something's there."

"That's what I thought. Which is why, on a whim, I left Eden a note."

Marcel blinked, slow and gentle, like his brain needed a second to catch up with her enthusiasm. "I'm trying to follow why you would do that? He said, eyes shining with delight.

Nothing romantic," she added quickly. "Just something to remind her she's seen. It worked so well I left another one. I was right there when she found it... and Marcel, I could see it *lifted* her."

Looking at her with a mix of amusement and admiration. "Are you telling me you're Eden's secret admirer? Like the Tooth Fairy but with stationery?"

Katy stalled with a couple of ums before blurting it out. "Okay, okay, I haven't figured out the whole job description yet, but here's the general idea. We offer a gentle nudge. Nothing big. Just enough to open Eden's heart."

"Open her heart to who? Donovan?"

"Yes! Come on now, you're starting to catch the vision! You and I can be the secret engines to make this happen. Kind of like undercover matchmakers."

"Undercover huh?" Marcel let his voice drop an octave lower. "I could stand to be under cover with you."

Katy coughed just to feel normal again. "Stay focused, sir."

His smile gentled his whole face, as if every line knew exactly how to welcome her in.

"Then we pivot. I've known Eden forever. I started out as her intern. I can tell something's shifting in her. It's like opening up, letting December work on her. I mean, with everything she's juggling, the holidays, her birthday coming up, work; it feels like she could use a little daily spark."

"And you want to make Donovan look like the sender."

"If it helps both of them? Abso-darn-lutely! You know him. I know her. It's perfect."

Marcel rubbed his chin thoughtfully. "You're really trying to orchestrate a tiny Christmas miracle, huh?"

Katy gave him the kind of raised eyebrow that could pass for a smirk. "Would that be so terrible?"

Marcel, he's grounded and tends to respond, not react. He understands people's rhythms. He's good at helping others feel safe to open up. He makes Katy feel like her ideas aren't "too much," which she finds... refreshing.

Shaking his head slowly, he said, "No, not all. It's not the worst idea I've heard."

Their server returned briefly with their drink order. Marcel thanked him, then turned his attention back to Katy, just in time for her gaze to drift across the room.

Through a decorative cut-out wall, Katy spotted him. Broad shoulders and the kind of easy grin that seemed to bend the air around him.

Leaning in close enough to flirt with committing to the bit, a woman touched his arm...he didn't pull away.

He seemed familiar. She recognized him immediately.

"Marcel," she whispered, "I think that's Christopher."

"Another man capturing your attention?"

"Yes, but not in the way you think. I think that's Christopher, the guy Eden's having coffee with tomorrow."

He was the same as Eden described and his picture confirmed.

Following her gaze, Marcel said, "So our date is turning into an episode of *The Flirtatious, Charming, and Possibly Dangerous.*"

"Possibly dangerous? That's adorable. You're barely PG-13. And relax. If anyone's at risk of being in danger here it's me. Have you seen yourself?"

Marcel grinned, captivated by her teasing.

"Hmm, he looks like a player." She said squinting.

"Huh? Even If that is the guy, they aren't exclusive. They just met. He's a single guy enjoying a night out. Why jump to player?"

"I have a sense about these things. And he's just a reminder why our secret admirer plan is necessary. I'm all for wanting Eden to have a Birthday-Bae but it has to be the *right* one."

"Hmm," Marcel teased. "I see. So, we're playing undercover matchmakers while also keeping Eden from getting played. This is a busy night for us."

"You seem to be catching on fast," Katy said smiling. "This is a fun challenge, but this is also us. We're getting ready to ensure all these love sparks land safely. Truly, you are the only person I'd want as my co-conspirator in love."

The waiter arrived with their piping hot entrees. Katy burned the roof of her mouth because patience was for people who didn't have THIS kind of food in front of them.

"You really think the chocolate bar gift today can change her life?"

"Not the chocolate per se", she said smirking. "The idea behind it. The message. It's about presence and intention. If we do this right," Katy paused to inhale more food. "It'll give her something meaningful every day.

The holiday musical selections for the evening were the perfect soundtrack for the holiday romance they were orchestrating.

"I'm not opposed to being your little partner in crime. Honestly, I wasn't going to say anything but I'm pretty sure Donovan is feeling Eden. But how long do you think we can pull this off? And what if Donovan finds out?"

"Let's take it day by day. We can make her birthday the finish line. If we make magic happen by then, we're legends. If not..."

The sentence trailed off, but the energy between them didn't.

Caught in the quiet thrill of a plan unfolding. Romance, friendship, mischief, it all blurred together.

Their eyes held just one beat too long.

Somewhere in the back of his mind, Marcel understood a single truth.

The sparks they were trying to orchestrate for Eden and Donovan were building right here. Between him and Katy where a December's kiss mirrored the moment.

Chapter 6

Running her fingers along the fabric, Eden frowned at her reflection, *"Does this say approachable, confident, mysterious, or just...cold?"*

The winter-white sweater sat against her chest like it was auditioning for a part she wasn't sure it could play. And the mirror didn't help. It only seemed to whisper more questions than answers.

She could almost hear Amara's voice yelling: "Girl, please pick something that doesn't scream, I overthink everything!"

Huffing and puffing aloud, Eden dropped the sweater onto the bed and reminded herself there were more important things to handle. The outfit could wait. The *assignment*, the one tucked inside her work bag...could not.

She reached in and pulled out the candy bar and the folded note. "If I'm going to do this, I might as well make it ceremonial."

Moving around her house with purpose, gathering what she needed:

· Her Bible

- ·   Her journal
- ·   A single candle
- ·   A playlist soft enough to make her think but warm enough to crack her open

She placed everything carefully on the coffee table with the chocolate bar centered like a sacred offering.

Folding her hands, she said, "All right. Let's do this."

Opening her bible to Hebrews 12:1, she read aloud: "*Therefore, since we are surrounded by such a great cloud of witnesses, let us throw off everything that hinders and the sin that so easily entangles. And let us run with perseverance the race marked out for us.*"

Closing the pages, she whispered, "Here goes nothing."

Slowly, she began speaking each word softly at first, like testing the waters.

"I lay aside and break every agreement I've made with old labels and negative storytelling."

The words felt strange on her tongue. Heavy, yet protective. Like dragging something she hadn't acknowledged before into the open. Closing her eyes, the candle smoke curled her like a soft shawl.

"I lay aside and break every self-imposed word I've spoken in fear."

Her voice grew steadier.

"I lay aside every past experience formed by trauma, caused by me or others and I place them at the feet of Jesus."

A shiver rippled through her. It wasn't cold, it was electricity, like something was being charged up. She pictured every doubt, every voice that'd ever tried to define her sliding off her shoulders and melting into the floorboards.

"I fall out of agreement with not being or having enough. I release any and everything that no longer serves me...like doves."

Visualizing the words lifting and taking flight, she smiled internally.

Her voice grew stronger, rising with each breath.

"And now, I take on and embrace Heaven's new name and identity for me and my life."

The room felt still, like it was listening.

And in the quiet, she heard herself say with confidence and conviction, "I'm not behind. I haven't missed my chance. I don't have to do this alone. In Jesus' name, may all these things be true."

In her mind's eye, heaven and earth met in agreement, like a divine handshake securing her future.

The words Laurence wrote, once seeming distant, now began to shimmer like the first trace of frost on a windowpane.

Eden closed her eyes again and saw herself running.

Free, light, focused, and joyful throwing off labels, expectations, and every story that ever tried to shrink her.

Her heart felt unburned, almost buoyant.

As if on cue, the candy bar tipped over with the gentlest thud.

"Is this...an invitation?"

Eden unwrapped it slowly, savoring the quiet sweetness, letting it melt, and smiling. The symbolic release was complete, but more than that, she could feel it. Her heart was prepared to receive whatever tomorrow might bring.

Before climbing into bed, she took one last look at herself in the mirror.

Tomorrow would bring coffee and conversations.

Tonight, brought transformation.

And that, Eden realized, was a gift all its own.

Chapter 7

Today was Christopher's date.

The past few days communicating with him were a breath of fresh air, for them both.

Still undecided on what to wear, Eden stretched beneath her duvet and weighted blanket. Both of which had conspired to trap her until noon.

This morning, she felt lighter. Not in the I went to Pilates twice in one day kind of way, but in the I finally put something down I didn't realize I was carrying way.

Blinking up at the ceiling, wondering if a full-on revival service had taken place in her living room the night before.

Her phone buzzed over on her nightstand.

Liora was calling.

Stretching and yawning, Eden answered, "Hey. It's kind of early for you. Everything okay?"

"Hey baby, her mother said, in the tone mothers reserve for when the Holy Spirit, gossip, and concern have formed a committee meeting. "I didn't want to wait too long to talk to you about this."

Sitting straight up, "Wait. That is not giving casual news."

"Marie called me last night."

Eden's heart didn't drop, exactly. It did however flicker.

"You mean... Boris' mother Marie?"

"Yes, *her*. That's the one. Old heifer."

"Oh." Eden swallowed. "Okay... but why would she be calling you?"

"I'm still trying to figure out why she felt the need to call *me,*" Liora said. "I don't know if she was bragging, *trying* to make me feel bad, or if she was genuinely happy and wanted to share the news with every contact in her phone."

"What did she want Mama? What did she say?"

Not wanting to say it just yet, Liora did a temperature check. "Have you heard anything about Boris lately?"

"Nope. Nothing at all."

"Well, I'm sorry sugar, this might not be easy to hear but she called to tell me her son got engaged last night."

"Boris got engaged last night?"

Boris Webb, the one Eden thought was the love of her life, her ex-fiancé. The one she'd given her whole heart to and thought she'd spend the rest of her life with. He'd just pledged and promised to another woman what he'd promised to her

For a moment, Eden didn't speak. She thought back on their lives together. She remembered Boris showing up for her in a way no one else ever had. That was the day she knew she could love him forever.

It'd been two years since she'd walked away and chosen herself.

Two years since she deleted, blocked, and erased every digital bread-crumb of Boris Webb from her life.

Two years since she told God she was done letting a man play tug-of-war with her heart.

Any other year? That news would've knocked the wind out of her, sending her spiraling into questions she had no business entertaining.

But today, it just landed. Not softly. Not harshly. Just... truthfully.

"Well," Eden said, exhaling slowly. "Isn't that something."

"You alright baby?" her mother asked.

"Honestly? Yeah, I think so." Eden pressed her palm to her chest. "Shocked? Yes. Is there a pinch of something sour there, sure. But I can tell you this, it's not devastation."

"Good, I'm glad. And guess what? You don't owe that man a single emotional penny. Him or his aggravating mama," Liora huffed. "But I did want to check in with you and tell you myself before you heard it somewhere else."

"I appreciate you, Mama." Eden said and she meant it.

It was clear, unforgiveness was loosening its grip on her without her permission.

"Now," Liora continued, shifting gears with Olympic-level skill, "don't you have your little coffee date today?"

"Mama, Eden exclaimed, "Why does it have be a *little* coffee date? She laughed.

"I'm just saying," her mother cut in. "And do *not* stay longer than ninety minutes. You know I stand firm in this teaching."

"You always say that."

"Because it works!" her mother snapped. "Ninety minutes. Let him leave wanting more, he doesn't need to know your whole life story. Give him a chance to want to see the sequel."

Eden bit her lip to keep from laughing. "Okay mama, I hear you."

"And Eden?"

"Yes?"

"Forgive yourself for whatever still stings. God already has."

Before Eden could absorb that, her phone beeped. Amara was video calling her.

"I heard the beep, go ahead and answer." Liora replied. "I'm sure it's Amara, calling to talk about your little date. Tell her I said hi. Call me later."

Eden switched over. Amara's face filled the screen like she'd been waiting to pounce.

"So, Amara said, eyes narrowing, "what are the outfit options? Because I know you're trying to figure out what to wear, like you're trying to solve the Da Vinci code in your closet."

Standing in front of her closet mirror, Eden held up three different outfits and zero clarity.

"Alright," Amara said, squinting. "Why do you look like you're auditioning for three different versions of yourself?"

Eden's phone beeped again.

"Hold on, it's Katy. Let me merge her in," Eden said.

The moment Katy appeared she didn't even greet her.

"Girl, put the green sweater back, it's giving Christmas at the bank."

"It's sage," Eden protested, holding it up.

"It's screaming savings account. Put it down now."

"Did you two call me to help or haunt me? Eden snorted.

"We *are* all the help you need," Katy said pointing her finger. "And not to mention, if you need a rescue excuse, text me our safe word. I'll call pretending your garage flooded or a raccoon broke into your closet."

"A raccoon Katy?" Eden laughed so hard. "Why a raccoon?"

"I don't know. That's the first thing that popped in my head. But I mean, now that I think about it, they *do* look like they steal breakthroughs."

All three women dissolved into laughter.

When the giggles settled, Eden took a breath. "Since y'all are in good spirits, I have some news I found out this morning."

"Oh? What'd you find out?" Amara asked.

"Boris got engaged last night."

"The Boris who swore to never speak of ever again in life Boris?" Amara's voice pitched higher with each word.

"Yes. That Boris. For whatever reason, his mother called mine last night to tell her."

Katy didn't say a word. She narrowed her eyes the way she did when she was mentally taking notes for later. She was gathering intel.

"With me, he said he needed freedom, Eden said softly. "He didn't want labels anymore. But now he's engaged. I guess he just needed to be free from me."

"No! Amara snapped. "You needed to be free from *him*. That ending wasn't a punishment, it was graduation. You were learning what you needed to learn. Now it's time to use it."

Amara continued on a roll. "And here's another thing, do not fear a blank page. That's where the best chapters are written. We wish him well, and we say good riddance. Now... what color are we wearing to meet Christopher?"

"Amara said everything I would've said," Katy nodded. "But Eden, you good? Really good?"

"Interestingly enough, I'm good. Yes, I was definitely shocked. But I did this little exercise last night where I released a whole bunch of stuff from my past. He said he needed freedom but, in a way, last night, I feel like I got it."

Katy didn't need to ask any follow up questions about the experiment because she knew all too well where it came from. She was happy her plan was working.

"Okay then," Amara declared. "So again. What color are we wearing?"

"What about this one?" Eden said holding up a cream sweater.

Both women shouted, "YES. THAT ONE."

"It's soft, wintery, and says 'I'm cute, I'm free, I'm single, but please don't act up because I have a gang of raccoons ready to fight,'" Amara added.

Their laughter filled Eden's home with warmth, real warmth, the kind that makes shadows lose their power.

"You got this Eden," Amara said.

"Now go and be cute, Katy added.

Chapter 8

S lipping into the cream sweater, the one her friends practically chose for her with prophetic authority, it hugged in all the right places. In the mirror, she didn't just see a woman getting ready for a date; she saw a woman who had survived herself. Somehow, she looked good doing it too. She truly did not look like what she'd been through.

When Christopher asked where they should meet. Eden chose her sanctuary: *Bean There, Filed That.* The café tucked into the first floor of her office building. A hidden gem. The kind of place with artisanal baked goods so good they bordered on spiritual warfare.

Arriving minutes early, she settled into a wooden corner table. Work was a shield for Eden, its familiarity wrapped around her like a soft throw blanket. No matter how the date went, she'd be close to home. Or least work, which was essentially the same thing.

The baristas were steaming homemade syrups, perfumed with vanilla, clove, and what she suspected was pure joy. Someone set out a tray of mini gingerbread donuts that probably violated a city ordinance on sugar entrapment.

Then Christopher walked in.

Charcoal coat. Easy smile. The kind of presence that made the whole room notice. He had the self-assured energy of someone who made complicated things run quietly and efficiently without demanding applause for it. An operations genius in the professional sports world, yes, but clearly a man who didn't mind living behind the curtain.

His eyes swept the room until they found her.

"Eden," he said, smiling as he approached.

"Hi," she replied, standing automatically and mirroring his smile without even trying.

Their hug wasn't tentative. It was familiar, like two souls who'd met somewhere else before agreeing to meet again in this lifetime.

They sat, and their world, their story...opened.

"You look very nice." Christopher said, leaning forward a little.

"Thank you. I had help."

His mouth curved. "I understand the statement. Women rarely reach this level of coordination without a committee."

"So, you're observant."

"I'm a middle child with two sisters. I know a collaborative effort when I see one. But yes, I am observant. Just like I *observed* you the other night."

For the first few minutes they talked the way new people talk, easy conversation, light jokes, small truths that feel big because they're shared with someone who's listening.

Then, quietly, it shifted into something deeper.

"How's your morning been?" Christopher asked.

Their drinks arrived. Eden's banana cream pie matcha latte smelled like dessert disguised as productivity. Christopher's hot Americano with two extra shots smelled like someone who took life seriously but not too seriously.

Eden set her cup down slowly, her fingers lingering on the warm ceramic.

"It's been. It's been...a morning," she said with a small laugh. "I actually found out something interesting earlier."

"Interesting?" He didn't flinch. He invited. Do you care to share?"

"Well," she said, drawing in a breath, "my ex got engaged last night."

Christopher blinked once. Not a deer-in-headlights blink but an "oh, I can hold space for this" type blink.

"Wow," he said. "That's a big thing to stumble into before 10 a.m., huh? How are you feeling about it?"

"Surprised, mostly. But also free in a way. Like a door closed and it didn't crush me on the way out."

"Good," he said gently. "You deserve that kind of peace."

She hadn't expected him to respond like that.

"Thank you for telling me," he added. "I know that couldn't have been easy to hear. Or easy to say."

"It wasn't," she admitted. "But somehow saying it hasn't ruined the day."

He smiled. "Well, I'll try my best not to ruin it either."

Time completely disregarded all laws of physics. Ninety minutes evaporated. Then another. Their coffee cooled., donuts disappeared, but their conversation didn't.

He asked about her work in public policy with genuine curiosity, not polite interest, not filler, but actual listening.

They traded stories about books they loved, foods they refused to negotiate, and the exact moment each realized adulthood was basically improvisation plus taxes. He told her about the time he tried to fix a sink and ended up flooding his neighbor's apartment. She shared the infamous raccoon rescue excuse Katy made up for her.

He laughed so hard he wiped tears.

Their little coffee date spilled out onto the decorated streets, talking like they were on chapter three of a story they didn't realize they were writing.

Lights draped every lamppost, glowing gold against the winter sky.

His arm brushed hers once. Then again. They stayed close enough that the space between them felt intentional.

When he suggested grabbing an early dinner, she didn't check her watch. Dinner was simply the next chapter in the day they were having.

It felt as if pulling away from each other would take actual effort. Neither one of them wanted the date to end.

They wandered through Christmas-lit streets, peppermint drifting from storefronts, the city softening around them into something gently blurred and quietly magical.

A door was opening for her, and she was stepping through it.

"So...there's this holiday work event I have to go to tomorrow evening," she said. "It's kind of a big deal in my line of work. Would you want to come with me?"

His eyebrows lifted with a playful glint. "I get to be your plus one?"

Something warm unfurled in her chest, it wasn't nerves, it was hope. She'd put these kinds of feelings aside after her breakup with Boris.

"I'd love to," he said without hesitation.

By the time the day finally wound down, sometime long after sunset, they reluctantly reached the moment where parting was the only option left.

"Text me when you get home," he said.

"Sure."

"And Eden?"

She paused looking up.

"That cream sweater," he said. "Excellent choice."

"Oh, thank you. My fashion board of directors' thanks you."

He chuckled, stepping back, giving her space, not hovering or rushing. "Thank you for an amazing day. Get home safe and enjoy the rest of your night."

"Thank you. I had a wonderful time too. I'll text you when I get home."

She was quite ready to let him know where she lived but she knew it wouldn't be long before they were communicating again because she was only seven minutes away.

What she didn't quite realize, at least not yet, was how forgiveness had quietly softened her. She walked home with her heart open just a little wider than before.

Chapter 9

Self-Care Sunday was supposed to be quiet and restful.

But Amara and Katy clearly had other plans because they burst through her door at 10:04 a.m. armed with fruit smoothies, healing bath salts, and matching pink "Self-Care Energy" tote bags. Each bag, stuffed with blush-toned essentials designed to crank up the frequencies of self-love.

"You're alive!" Katy shouted.

She is alive!" Amara added like they'd just spotted a rare bird.

"I think I may need to get my key back." Eden shared.

"Nah, this belongs to me. Try and get it back if you want to." Amara continued.

"I texted you both back," Eden protested weakly.

"Seven hours later," Katy's tone suggested a felony.

"And only four words," Amara added. "*'The date went well.'* Totally unacceptable. An absolute crime."

"An absolute crime," Katy agreed. "And I, for one, want reparations."

Eden sighed but smiled. "Come on in and I'll give you all the details."

They settled into the living room. Candles lit, robes on, hair tied up like a spiritual council preparing for an important summit. Amara hopped onto the couch with both legs tucked beneath her like she was settling in for a sermon. Katy sat cross-legged on the floor like a camp counselor about to hand out instructions.

"Okay," Eden said, holding her Bahama Mama smoothie like it was a mic. "So... he is simply perfect."

Their shrieks could have cracked drywall.

Katy slapped the pillow beside her. "What do you *mean* perfect? I'm sure you've lived long enough to know nobody's perfect, even the perfect looking."

"I mean, Eden said, searching, "he...saw me." She couldn't explain it any better.

"And did he look good?" Katy asked.

"Ridiculously," Eden answered. "He came in wearing this charcoal coat, smiling like he was heaven sent."

"Amen," Katy whispered reverently.

"And," Eden added, a little breathless, "I invited him to the holiday party tonight."

There was a stunned pause.

Then a scream that probably scared every bird in the city.

Amara grabbed her hand. "So, you're telling me Christopher might actually be—"

"Birthday-Bae," Eden finished. "And guess what? He's in his Jubilee season, too. He turned fifty a few months ago and celebrated in Africa."

Katy leaned back for dramatic effect. "Oh, I see. He's a go-big-or-go-home type man, huh?"

"He's... possible," Eden admitted soft and honest.

The room warmed around that sentence.

And then Katy clapped her hands once, which sounded dangerous.

"Alright. If we're talking possibilities, we're cleaning house."

"What?" Eden asked.

"We are not going to allow you to enter into Jubilee with Boris' spirit still lingering around. So today, we purge."

It started small.

Amara found a shoebox under Eden's bed labeled *Miscellaneous*.

"Miscellaneous?" Katy said. "Open it."

Inside: cards from every holiday and just because from Boris. Handwritten notes. Ticket stubs from concerts. Old pictures from photo booths.

Katy dropped it all into the burn bowl like she was banishing monsters.

Next came the clothes he'd gifted her and a pair of earrings he'd purchased on a trip to Charlotte.

"You didn't even like those earrings, why are you still holding onto them? Amara asked.

"They made my ears itch," Eden admitted. "Who knows."

"Into the burn bowl," Katy commanded. "What else? Do we need to burn? Do you have old voicemails? Texts? Let's clear the inbox while we're at it."

Scrolling through her phone, there was one voicemail she never deleted. It was the last she had of his voice.

"Don't even play it Eden. Just delete it. Katy said."

She hit delete and the message vanished forever.

Every item felt like a tiny fracture closing.

A framed photo found its way out of a drawer. It was their last trip together.

Eden stared at it for a long enough for the room to compress and expand.

"You okay?" Katy asked, softer now.

Nodding slowly, Eden said, "Yeah. I just needed to see the face of the woman I *used* to be. And tell her she's free."

She placed the photo in the burn bowl herself.

Katy struck the match with a flourish. The flame licked the paper; a sigh of smoke rose. And for a second, the little pieces of Eden's past flew like fragile birds. The symbolism wasn't lost on her and landed like a benediction.

The warmth of the flames reflected on her face as the fire devoured the paper and fabric, while the ash smelled like finality.

As her love life crackled and collapsed in front of her she whispered a truth meant only for herself to hear, "*I let go and burn away every disappointment.*" She thought.

"Okay," Katy said after the last curl of smoke. "Glad we got that out of the way. Now it's time to rest. Resting is also a part of self-care Sunday."

Which translated to blankets, hot tea, facemasks, and thirty minutes of lying quiet while the three of them processed the moment.

None of them had felt this clear in years. Eden's purging somehow lightened them too.

By late afternoon they migrated back to her room like a glam squad on assignment.

Because tonight?

Tonight was another date.

A big one.

Tonight, she would enter a room filled with important players in her world. And when she entered, she wasn't walking in with old weight and stagnated energy.

No, she was walking in with new light and heaven help anyone who tried to dim it.

Chapter 10

The ballroom looked like appropriated budget money found its way into a tuxedo.

Crystal chandeliers glittered like suspended galaxies. Servers glided between political socialites holding trays of things most people found hard to pronounce but enjoyed anyway.

A twelve-piece jazz ensemble leaned into a silky-smooth rendition of "This Christmas," and no one was doing the most, yet everyone absolutely was.

Eden arrived at the venue wrapped in holiday glamour, the deep, sparkly incarnation of Christmas. A deep merry merlot satin slip dress layered under a long very vanilla colored wool coat, that moved like its own quiet entrance theme. Her short curls were brushed into soft, defined waves, framing her face. Pinned on one side with a jeweled barrette that caught the light every time she turned. The faintest sweep of gold shimmer dusted her collarbone.

Inside, the low thrum of impressive people, impressive mingling clustered around draped high-top cocktail tables, this was the kind of place where one strategic hello could shift an entire quarter.

Katy and Marcel caught up to Eden, greeting colleagues and collecting compliments like polite little trophies.

Katy immediately grabbed Eden's hand and said, "But can we acknowledge your waistline is evangelizing tonight."

"Ahh, thanks Katy, you and Marcel both look lovely too." Eden said smiling.

Marcel nodded reverently, "Amen."

Already inside, Christopher spotted them.

He paused, mid-conversation. His eyes softened, taking Eden in with a look that might've been a prayer if anyone examined it too closely.

Eden felt it, the pull of a gaze worthy of making a room disappear.

Christopher approached like she was the only person there.

"Okay, so he looks like he owns stock in handsome," Katy whispered, fanning herself in chiffon.

"I can hear you, Katy," Marcel deadpanned.

"Oh honey, let's not get it twisted. You are the major stockholder of handsome. He only owns a few shares." Katy said quickly trying to recover.

Marcel pointed, "Oh look, there's Donovan."

Entering in through the east entrance, graphite was his color choice for the evening, paired with a port-colored tie making him look like a Christmas catalog model. that made him look like the models in the Christmas catalogues. And the woman on his arm matched his catalog vibes.

His date, Lena, a chic and stylish policy analyst, stood beside him in a sleek, cookie-crumb colored sequined jumpsuit, sipping sparkling cider with easy confidence.

Eden recognized her from past events.

Something tugged at Eden unexpectedly, a quick pinch behind her heart. It wasn't jealousy. It was as if she'd never quite looked at him long enough to notice how magnetic he truly was.

Eden's attention sharpened to where Donovan noticed her attention.

His expression lifted. It wasn't longing. Perhaps something harder to name. Awareness, maybe.

He offered a polite smile. She gave a polite smile back.

She didn't linger. Especially since Christopher was standing in front of her saying, "You look..." He stopped, to reevaluate and recalibrate. "Unreal."

"Oh my God, you look incredible," he added, taking her hands as if he'd been waiting all night.

"So do you," she said. "Velvet? Now that's a bold choice."

"It's the holidays. I figured I'd try and match the decor."

She laughed, and something about the way he looked at her made the laughter soften into something slower, almost deferential.

"Christopher, allow me to introduce you. This is Katy and Marcel."

"Oh. Katy? Raccoon Katy?" Christopher asked scanning for confirmation.

"You told him that?!" Katy bit towards Eden before admitting, "That would be me. She and I are one in the same."

"Well, it's nice to meet you, Katy." He said extending a hand.

"And nice to meet you too, man," Christopher said acknowledging Marcel with that easy, unspoken man to-man nod.

The two couples drifted into the flow of the evening, holiday greetings, networking, the kind of subtle hand on the back moments that made Eden's pulse do light cardio.

Katy and Marcel broke away, stationing themselves ten feet away, posing as sociable while operating full surveillance.

Eden shot them a look promising a later confrontation.

For an hour, everything felt dreamy. Warm and easy. Like a night eager to be remembered.

But the rhythm of the evening hiccupped when Christopher's phone could not escape the incessant vibrations buzzing around in his pocket. The calls and texts kept coming. Hard. Urgent.

Unable to ignore, he stepped away to take the calls with a mixture of annoyance and professionalism.

Returning, his expression said everything.

"I'm so sorry, he said returning. "There's a real work emergency I have to attend to. Not a fake one so I can leave early. I don't have a gang of raccoons waiting for me. Although Katy might be right about them stealing breakthroughs."

Eden was used to disappointment. She thought she'd purged those old patterns and gotten rid of the negative stories.

The raccoon reference softened the sting.

"I understand," she said. And she did. She was in her world tonight. This was his. He was needed elsewhere.

"I hate leaving you. But I promise I'll make this up to you." He said, daring to seal his proclamation with a soft kiss to her lips.

"I know."

Kissing her forehead this time, prolonging his stay just a little longer. He squeezed her hand one last time...and left.

Observing from a distance, Katy and Marcel watched the scene unfold as Eden stood alone in a room full of people.

"Well, well, well. Didn't see this coming. I wonder what happened." Katy whispered to Marcel.

Eden exhaled and steadied herself. Where would she go next? She even considered leaving early herself. But her boss, Thomas and his wife intercepted. Introducing her to someone, keeping her anchored in the evening.

A stir at the entrance caused the temperature to rise ten degrees in a heartbeat.

There were whispers.

Applause.

Camera flashes going off like firecrackers.

A few people straightened as if they'd been asked to stand for the pledge.

Eden followed the ripple of attention.

There, she saw them.

Or rather, *him*.

After self-care Sunday, what are the chances she would see....

BORIS.

With his fiancé. A newly elected congresswoman from another state. She was newly important, newly everything. Her holiday attire, sharp yet tasteful. Her posture stiff, a calculated smile trying too hard.

"Oh no," Katy whispered. "Now this is either a plot twist or character development."

Fully invested in Eden's story, Marcel said, "Hey, what's happening here? What's the commotion about with these two?"

Katy updated Marcel with all of the Boris and Eden lore.

"Oh wow, should we go over to her?"

"No, not yet. I think I want to see how this is going to play out. Man, that lady looks like she's allergic to happiness and irons her socks."

Marcel nearly chocked on his sparkling cider, "Katy, be nice."

"Oh, trust me, this is me being nice," Katy muttered. "In my head I said much worse."

Eden inhaled slowly. She had already forgiven him. She had already released it but actually seeing him with her in real life.

It definitely stung a little bit.

She wasn't alone for long.

Of course, Boris saw her.

He always saw her just not when; she needed him to.

He approached with the familiar confidence of someone who assumed the door to her heart would stay unlocked for him.

"Eden," he said. "Wow, you look...gorgeous. How've you been?"

Two years later, she looked radiant. He looked...aged.

"Thank you," she replied, polite but stern. "I've been well. And I hear congratulations are in order for you."

His smile tightened. "I see mama is still running her mouth. Yeah...about that."

And just like that, this man had the audacity.

"It's not what it looks like," he murmured. "It's politics. Strategy. Optics. You know the deal."

She blinked once. "It looks to me like you're getting married."

"Yeah, I know, but not how you think."

"Boris, marriage is not a prop," she said, trying to keep her voice low. "Is that what it means to you? You and I were engaged. Was I a prop too?"

He examined her face like he was searching for old echoes. "It's... not like that, Eden."

Stepping in closer he said, "I've tried calling and sending texts, but I figured you had me blocked. I figured you didn't want to hear from me. Yes, I moved away but I never stopped thinking about you. I never got a chance to explain. This is going to sound harsh but at the time, you didn't fit the brand I was building. I felt like I had no choice."

Eden's jaw line tightened. "Your brand? Are you serious? You always had a choice. You just didn't choose me."

He exhaled, frustrated, reaching for her elbow as if that would help. "Listen. I only came here tonight because I knew I would see you. Eden, I still love—"

"Shut up. No, you don't," she said sharply. "You love the version of me totally sold out to you. And I don't want your kind of love. Your love hurts."

Stunned by Eden's admission, he opened his mouth, but nothing came out. What could? Her words gutted him.

It was like, she used to know Boris. Two years later, he was almost a stranger.

Stepping in closer and reaching for her again, he said, "Let's go somewhere where we can talk. We had something real. I still feel it, and I know you do too."

Pulling away sharply, he grabbed her.

"I thought you'd wait for me," he said.

Eden shot him an icy stare, "I did. Then I didn't."

Donovan appeared lipping between them like a calm shield. Like it was the most natural thing in the world, Donovan asked, "Everything alright here?"

"This is a private conversation." Boris said.

"Are you good?" Donovan asked Eden, his eyes on her, not on Boris.

"Yes," she said. And she was. Because he was here.

Boris stepped forward again. "I said, this is a private conversation."

Boris' fiancé glanced over from the other side of the room, clearly sensing drama brewing.

"Maybe it was," Donovan said calmly, "But it's not anymore because I've joined it."

Katy and Marcel still watching the scene unfold like they were at the movie theaters, narrated with glee.

"He's standing really close," Katy said.

"Okay, Donovan...my man. Way to stand up for your lady." Marcel replied back with enthusiasm.

"Oh, I like this for her. I like it a lot." Katy squealed.

And Eden?

She wasn't sure what she liked.

Except she knew she was grateful for the way God rearranged a night that could have potentially been ruined.

Boris looked at Eden, waiting.

She spoke clearly, "We're done here, Boris. Seriously. Enjoy your *freedom*. And have a happy life."

There was something in the way she spoke, Boris knew Eden meant what she said.

He hesitated, then walked back to his 'fiancé.'

The second he was out of earshot, Eden let out a breath she didn't know she'd been holding.

"Are you okay?" Donovan asked, holding her up.

She nodded. "Thank you."

"I didn't do much."

"You did enough."

His smile tugged softly, as if her answer landed somewhere he wasn't expecting.

Donovan didn't look away from Eden. "Come on. Let's get you some fresh air. Figuratively because it's cold outside or some cake. I think cake seems to fix everything."

For the rest of the evening Donovan stayed close, like her personal bodyguard. Lena, his date caught his eye from across the room and gave a tiny, encouraging nod before returning to her conversation. She understood what was happening.

They settled at a high-top table near the band.

"You know, I've been meaning to reach out to you about your take on the projection inconsistencies."

"So why haven't you? We were supposed to set up some time to discuss scalability."

"You know, time is moving fast and slipping away."

"But you know. You can call me anytime."

Donovan's invitation for a call felt more personal than professional.

"Sure, I can do that."

Katy and Marcel watched the Donovan and Eden show with satisfaction.

Christopher swept her in with sparkle. Boris tried to tug her back.

And Donovan simply showed up.

Chapter 11

Monday morning arrived too early and too bright, the kind of morning that had the nerve to be cheerful while Eden was still sorting through the emotional hangover of the weekend.

Slipping through her office doors, she braced herself in the event a mysterious gift might be present.

Flicking on the office lights, she scanned every surface.

Her desk? Empty.

The chair? Empty as well.

The windowsill? Tragically empty.

The plant corner? Only the fiddle-leaf, judging her like it knew she'd been expecting something.

There were no gifts.

"Girl, really?" she whispered to herself. "You didn't even believe in this days ago. Now you're searching?"

But the truth nudged her. For the "I'll take care of it" queen the mystery was intriguing. Maybe because mystery required nothing of her. No thank-you card, no humility speech, no "you didn't have to do this."

The real truth: she was beginning to understand receiving. Not the old habits of pushing help away or acting like her joy needed to be earned with receipts and hard work.

"Good morning, my darlin", Katy sang, sliding in dramatically with two lattes, shutting the door with her foot. "I've been waiting ALL night to talk about what in the gospel according to policy love happened last night."

"Katy –" Eden groaned.

"Oh yes, we are absolutely recapping."

Katy plopped into the visitor chair and crossed her legs like she was settling in for a Sunday morning service.

"So," she said, eyes bright, "how are you feeling after the most unpredictable weekend ever?" Setting Eden's drink down like a bribe.

"Oh my God, like seriously the most unpredictable weekend." Eden echoed.

"So, let's review, shall we? Katy held up an imaginary clipboard. Self-care Sunday was a whole blessing, we released and felt lighter. You looked AH-MAZING, and just in time to BAM, run into Boris and his make-believe fiancé looking like a clearance-rack political power couple."

"Katy." Eden chuckled, nodding solemnly, as if someone invoked the name of a defeated villain. The Ghost of Bad Decisions Past."

"No shade," Katy said raising her hand. "Okay, well, maybe a little shade."

Leaning back, Eden said, "Honestly? I'm not sure how I feel. It's like, I feel like I've been releasing all of this old stuff. Like I really thought I was done. Like *done* done. Then out of nowhere everything happened at once."

"What are you talking about? You are done," Katy said. "But your spirit needed feedback."

"Feedback?"

"Yes, Eden feedback. You purge something and life says, "Oh cool, you sure? Your spirit needed to see how you'd respond. Think of it like a pop quiz. Not meant to ruin your G.P.A., just check your progress. As far as I could tell, you passed."

"Well, I can tell you this. I almost cussed Boris' you-know-what-out-last-night."

"That would have been protective edification, and he would have earned every one of those beautiful choice words. Oh, but the real storyline of the night? Mr. Donovan stepped in like a whole Avenger, dripped out in graphite.

Eden couldn't help but laugh, "Yes, he sure did."

"That man swooped in like a protective shield. You said you were going to call him about the inconsistences in the project. But I think you should call him because fate deserves a fighting chance. Katy said nudging Eden's knee.

A soft knock interrupted them.

The receptionist stood there holding a box, beautifully packaged in moss green paper and tied with a cream silk ribbon.

"For you, Eden," she said.

Sitting up straight, Eden confirmed, "For me?"

The receptionist nodded, "Yep. Has your name on it," and left.

Katy lit up like she had front-row seats to destiny. "Open it," she whispered.

Eden set the box on her desk and untied the ribbon carefully. Peeling back the paper, her breath hitched.

Inside was a full ceremonial-grade matcha set. Bamboo whisk, stone-green bowl, a tin of rare, shade-grown matcha. And a handwritten note tucked at the bottom.

The card read:

Receive with intention. Make something slowly and let it nourish you. No earning. No apologizing. Just receive.

There was no signature.

A mysterious gift still showed up.

"Girl!" Eden exclaimed. "Christopher came through FAST."

"Christopher?" Katy asked, trying and failing to sound casual.

Eden's cheeks warmed. "It has to be from him, right? After last night? Like...his way of making up for leaving early? He knows it's my favorite drink from Saturday."

"Or...."Katy said dramatically, "maybe it's from Donovan. If you remember, you were drinking matcha during the meeting. Remember? Men remember more than we give them credit for."

Eden was already feeling herself leaning towards Christopher as the sender. But she couldn't ignore the fact Donovan does notice details in the way he rescued her last night.

Either way she liked the feeling.

Her phone buzzed.

Christopher's name lit up.

"Speak of the maybe gift giver and he shall appear," Eden said eyes widening.

Katy stayed rooted to the chair, she did not excuse herself as she normally would. Her thumbs flying as she texted Marcel a detailed narration.

She answered smiling, "Good morning."

"Morning," he said, his voice warm and scratchy, like he'd just finished a long night with short sleep. "I was just thinking about you and wanted to call and check in."

"I'm good, how are you?"

"Tired," he admitted. "But it comes with the territory. You had your matcha yet, I might need to get some. I have another long day today."

Eden's eyes flew to Katy when she mouthed, "OH MY GOD, HE SAID MATCHA," flailing silently.

Katy nodded but very much invested.

"I remember you ordered it the other day," Christopher continued, "and explained ceremonial grade and how it offered you time-released energy. I think I might have to convert."

Eden wasn't sure what to do with the fact he remembered that much.

"Well...yes. I have had my matcha. Katy surprised me with a latte this morning.

Clearing his throat, Christopher said, "I...I really meant what I said last night. I owe you a proper dinner. I was hoping to make it up to you tonight. No interruptions this time."

"That sounds nice," she said, with warmth blooming through her. "I'd love to."

"Great, I'll text you the details later. Enjoy the rest of your day. Goodbye."

"Wonderful, I look forward to it." Eden said.

Suddenly feeling brave from her successful call with Christopher, Eden picked up her phone.

"I'm going to call Donovan," she said.

"For the project," Katy added, eyebrows raised.

"Well obviously." Eden smirked.

Dialing. He answered on the second ring.

"Good morning, Eden," he said steady as always. "How are you after such an eventful evening.?"

"Recovering and ready to get back to work."

They talked about the revitalization initiative, the budget gaps, and a few policy angles they'd both been studying. There was an ease in their conversation, a growing familiarity.

She felt it. He certainly did.

They didn't flirt. They didn't need to.

His steadiness was its own invitation.

"Would you mind if I stopped by your office to talk timelines?" Donovan asked.

"Sure, that would be great. I have a mid-afternoon opening."

A soft, charged pause settled between them. The kind that comes right before a spark catches fire.

"Perfect," he said. "I'll see you soon,"

Eden hung up and exhaled.

"Baby, Monday is trying to romance you." Katy said already texting Marcel the latest update.

And for the first time, in a long time, Eden let herself receive that.

Chapter 12

Unsure how many times a woman could float, Eden was beginning to wonder if the Lord was testing her limits with gravity.

Christopher had been intentional all day. Small texts, thoughtful little check-ins, little "I'm looking forward to tonight" messages that makes a woman feel chosen, not chased.

This particular Monday did not have the Monday blues. No, it had Eden feeling like a walking Psalms 37:4, in the flesh.

Her meeting with Donovan was sublime and wildly productive.

Wrapped in a pressed camel colored sweater dress with the matching coat, draped her like a blessing.

Her Uber driver slowed as it approached the restaurant.

There he stood. Christopher. Looking like God took his time shaping every detail making him. Already on time. And not that pretend, performative kind either. This was the, *"I respect your time because I respect you."*

Stepping out of the car, he stepped forward to intercept her.

"Hello there, he said, eyes warming. "You look beautiful."

"And you look like you're up to something." She said teasing and taking his hand as she slid out of the seat.

"Maybe," he grinned. But good somethings."

Inside, he opened the door, with faithful conviction and walked beside her with full presence. And for a moment, she stood there receiving – his attention, his presence, and the way he made space for her without making a show of it.

The restaurant was the kind that acted like it was doing you a favor by handing you a menu. Eden smiled. She'd mentioned liking their salmon once while on their date.

And this man remembered.

It felt like God Himself signed off on the reservation.

Their hostess led them through the elegant section of the dining room, then suddenly turned a corner, into what could only be described as wall-to-wall screens glimmering like Time Square clothed in sports jerseys.

Professional football on a Monday night, electrified with pre-play-off energy. Head-to-head basketball action on the next. And another screen cycling through sports highlights, news, and commentary from big media personalities.

And right above their table?

A countdown clock for the second quarter.

Pulling her chair out, she sat blinking slowly.

Once she was seated, he blinked faster.

"Oh," he said, smiling a little too wide. "Okay. This isn't quite where I thought we'd be seated." As the hostess placed two menus in front of them, blissfully unaware of the spiritual warfare currently brewing."

"Enjoy," she chirped, then disappeared like a feather in the wind.

"I…I swear I didn't plan this," he said leaning in. "I promise I wasn't even thinking about any kind of games tonight."

Lifting her eyebrow, she said, "You sure? I mean, this *is* your world. Your bread and butter."

Laughing and dropping his head, he said, "True, true this is how the bills get paid. But I'm serious. I wanted tonight to be…about us."

And he meant it. She could tell. The way he was fighting for eye contact was almost adorable. Every touchdown and every three-point replay put Eden in her own sport's competition.

He was caught between a rock and a highlight reel.

"So, it looks like we are…in the middle of a sports cathedral, huh?"

Feeling defeated he said, "I'm so sorry."

She breathed slowly, feeling a new awareness. This was one of those moments where receiving wasn't simple and sweet. Sometimes receiving means saying what you need instead of pretending you don't have any.

She didn't want to compete. Not tonight.

"Christopher."

Looking up soft and attentive, he answered, "Yes Eden."

"Hey, listen I know you didn't pick this section. And I also know you love sports. I'm not interested in feeling like I'm battling with a scoreboard all night either. Maybe, I'll just --."

"And you won't," he said, interjecting quickly. "Hold on. Give me a minute/ Let me fix it."

Waving down a hostess with the urgency of a man calling for healing at a tent revival, he said, "Excuse me ma'am? Is there a chance we can move to a quieter section. We didn't realize how…immersive this area was."

Glancing around the glowing sports extravaganza for the first time like she was seeing it through their eyes. "Oh sure, let me see what I can do."

Within minutes, she whisked them to a cozy corner with one muted television far in the distance, more decorative than distracting.

Settling in she said, "I really appreciate this, Christopher." She told him.

"No seriously, I appreciate you for saying something and telling me. I really want to be present this evening. I like you, Eden. A lot."

Blushing she said, "I like too."

The night finally began to flow and find its rhythm. Their conversations opened like flowers in warm light. He asked thoughtful questions. She shared pieces of herself normally tucked away. They laughed, like real laughter.

Reaching over to grab her hand, his thumb brushed along her hand, "I'm really glad we moved." He shared.

"Yeah." she said, meeting his eyes. "Me too."

"And for the record," he added. "Had we stayed in that section, I would've been looking at you more than the games."

"Is that right? Now you want to take credit for the temptation you avoided?"

Grinning he said, "Well, a man can try, right?"

By dessert, Eden received a download.

Receiving isn't about everything going right. It's about allowing someone to show you who they are and you deciding how to respond.

Christopher showed her a man who listened, adjusted, and willing to course-correct and cared enough to protect the moment between them.

And she received that. Fully.

Chapter 13

Tuesday arrived without drama, which somehow, felt suspicious.

Eden woke up lighter than she had in weeks. Not quite euphoric but ... clear. Like someone opened a window overnight and let fresh air do what it does best. Though at thirty degrees, that definitely didn't happen for real.

By mid-morning, she was halfway through her emails when a small box was delivered once again by the receptionist.

Eden stared at the box and then at the receptionist.

"Of course," she whispered. "Because why wouldn't this keep happening."

"I'll leave you to it," the receptionist said walking away.

The glossy blush wrapping paper and satin ribbons were so pretty. The packaging wasn't flashy. It was, however, soft and thoughtful.

Inside was a bubble bath set so beautiful it felt unnecessary in the best way. A pale pink bottle. A plush white towel folded like it belonged in a spa commercial. And tucked between them, a clear glass bubble wand.

Eden's eyelids fluttered in surprise.

Then she laughed.

At the bottom of the box rested a small card.

Day 7 – Restore your joy. Today, do something playful. Something that brings you pure delight. Joy is holy, so let yours rise.

She held the card to her chest for a moment longer than necessary.

"Wow," she said with her voice low. "Joy."

She said the word again and again, "Joy."

She wasn't wondering about logistics anymore and how it got there or who sent it, she was simply grateful to receive it.

***

Across town, Marcel leaned against the edge of his desk with his jacket off and his tie loosened, scanning a report while Donovan stood nearby sipping coffee.

"Hey, did you see the email about that foundation's hosting a toy giveaway this weekend?" Marcel asked.

"Hmm, I don't think so. I get so many foundation requests, which one?" Donovan replied.

Marcel named it. One they'd both partnered with before. Solid, community-rooted work. Policy-adjacent enough to matter.

"Oh and," Marcel added. "They need volunteers for gift wrapping this week and for the event itself. You interested?"

"Send me the details," Donovan said. "I'll check my schedule and see where I can help."

Marcel switched his tone somewhat like they were about to have their own private locker room briefing.

"If it'll help with your schedule, I think Eden will be there."

"Eden?" Donovan paused. "Why would she matter in my decision-making process?"

"Oh, so we're going to act like you haven't been noticing her lately?" Marcel teased. "Is that what we're doing these days man?"

Donovan didn't look up right away. He finished his sip and set his cup down.

"Oh yeah, I've noticed." He said evenly.

That was it. No follow-up. No explanation. Just acknowledgment.

Marcel nodded once, satisfied, like that was the point of the entire conversation.

Smiling to himself as Donovan walked away, Marcel sent Katy a text:

Phase one √

***

On the other side of town, Katy practically vibrated, realizing she was up next.

Stepping into the frame of Eden's open door, eyes sparkling with the dangerous energy of a woman who had a plan and zero intention of asking permission.

Before you say no," Katy said. "I need you to say yes."

"To what?" Eden asked cautiously.

"Toy wrapping."

"Say what now, Katy?"

"Toy. Wrapping. Eden," Katy repeated, like she was speaking to a child. "Did you not see the email about the foundation hosting the giveaway? They need volunteers and I signed us up. Marcel will be there. Donovan is involved. You know, our peeps. It'll be fun."

Staring at Katy, Eden said, "You know how much work I have going on right now. As much as I'd love to, I'm too busy. I have several things I'm trying to wrap up before Christmas break."

"Eden, I know you're busy. We're all busy. But sometimes doing things for others helps us. Not to mention, you love kids. You love service. And wrapping toys for children screams, Joy to the World!"

Struck by Katy's use of the word, joy, Eden looked at her suspiciously.

"Why would you say *Joy to the World*? I mean like out of all of the songs, why that one?" Eden said zeroing in Katy.

Feeling Eden's heat, Katy bounced back, intentionally, trying to throw Eden off her instincts, "Because joy to the world, the Lord has come, duh. C'mon, it's Christmas time. Work will always be here."

Eden opened her mouth to protest. Only nothing came out. Deep down, she knew Katy was right. And right on cue, she remembered today's assignment: to curate joy today.

In an act of surrender, she said, "Fine, but I'm not wearing an elf hat."

Beaming, Katy said, "We'll see."

***

After a long day at the office, it was only logical for Eden to run a hot bath. She felt the longing of the old commercial, "Calgon, take me away."

Reaching for her latest gift, steam filled her bathroom, fogging the mirror.

She poured the bubble bath generously, watching the water cloud and bloom. For the sake of kicks and giggles, she indulged and dipped the bubble wand into the growing bath as the bubbles rose.

Lifting it slowly, reminiscent of her childhood, she smiled and blew.

A bubble landed on her nose and popped.

Truly tickled by the moment, she carefully undressed, shedding the day piece by piece.

Standing there bare, meeting her own reflection, Eden felt something sacred.

She felt joy without purpose. Peace without productivity.

Sinking into the tub, surrounded by bubbles and candles, and soft music, she allowed herself to be delighted without explanation. It was clear, joy is never anything that has to be earned.

Later, wrapped in her robe, phone buzzing nearby, Eden checked to find the volunteer confirmation email.

She smiled softly.

Whatever was unfolding and whoever was part of it, she trusted this much: Joy was returning. And it was making room for something good.

Chapter 14

This Wednesday arrived like the kind of morning that whispered, *today will be a good day*. Fifteen days from Christmas, and twenty days from her birthday.

Time was either winding down or tightening up. Eden felt the duality of both.

Laurence's letter lay on the nightstand, purposely placed where it rested since the first night. A few of the words seemed to call out for a review:

In the days to come, doors will begin to open for you, doors you thought were forever closed. Trust the process, trust yourself, and trust the One who's never left your side.

Eden smiled, grateful not just for the letter but for the unfolding adventure. Katy encouraged her to treat each gift and assignment like a Jubilee advent calendar but interestingly, it felt like it was sprinkled with the mischief of an Elf on a Shelf. And Eden, for the most part had.

The receptionist had been delivering the last set of gifts but each day entering her office, she still approached her office with high alert.

Stepping inside, her eyes landed immediately on the day's gift.

A new box. A new gift. Possibly a new revelation.

Allowing her joy to rise, what would today's gift box hold?

Inside, a single ink pen rested atop a small card:

Day 8 – Gratitude. Today, write 50 things you are grateful for. Let your heart speak freely; notice, name, receive.

While her day was scheduled with back-to-back meetings. Gratitude wasn't a to-do-list. It wasn't transaction. It was a magnet for miracles. And today, meetings could wait while she indulged in a deliberate pause.

Claiming her favorite nook by her office window, sunlight, slanted across her desk. Flexing her fingers around the new pen, the first ten items came easy.

By twenty, her mind slowed. The exercise now required more focus. She found herself jotting the small things she rarely noticed.

At number twenty-seven surprisingly, revelation peeked through. The chaos of her overthinking forced her to see patterns, people, and herself differently.

By number thirty, she paused and inhaled. Coming up with fifty things to be grateful for was a little more difficult than she expected. However, she figured, this gratitude exercise was not for approval, it was purely hers.

A ping from her calendar reminded her to step back into the day's rhythm as a notification for her first meeting popped up. She made a quiet vow. She would return to the list before the day ended.

A lunchtime check-in from Christopher mixed up the monotony of the day.

"How's your day going today lovely?" he asked.

"It's...busy, but I'm grateful." She said with a small smile tugging at her lips.

"I hear that," he said. "And are you still planning to do the gift-wrapping event later?"

"Yes sir, that's still the plan." She replied.

"It sounds like fun; I would've loved to join you guys. But duty calls," he said. "Save all the stories and fill me in later."

Imagining Christopher in a tiny elf hat, somehow made her grateful all over again.

"Oh, I just had a thought. Maybe I can join you guys for the actual event?" Christopher suggested.

"You know what? That's sounds like a good idea. I like that." Eden replied.

And just like that another date between Christopher and Eden was set.

By late afternoon, the office day finally tapered down. Katy burst into Eden's office like a hurricane on heels.

"You like my gift-wrapping outfit? Are you ready to have some fun? You, me, Marcel, Donovan...we're essentially the dream team. Joy to the world, Eden! Let's go." Katy said.

"Let me change really quick." Eden said, already smiling at the chaos she felt was coming.

Minutes later, decked in festive, still functional attire, Katy handed Eden an elf hat.

"I told you I wasn't wearing that."

"You are," Katy said, waiving it with the persistence of someone who knows better than you.

Eden slowly took the hat, then let it perch jauntily on her head.

"Happy now?"

"Yes ma'am and I think you are too." Katy said as they walked out of the door.

Chapter 15

The foundation's warehouse smelled like paper, tape, and the faint promise of holiday magic.

The room was a hive of activity, volunteers hustling between tables piled high with gifts, ribbons spilling everywhere like colorful confetti, and the slight strains of Christmas music looping overhead.

Volunteer groups from other organizations and companies were grouped together wrapping gifts.

Katy and Eden walked through the groups, finding their way to Donovan and Marcel.

"Katy. Eden. Over here!" Marcel called out. "Y'all ready to wrap some joy?"

Adjusting her elf hat, Eden said, "I'm ready. It's looking a little like organized madness in here."

"Organized madness, huh?" Marcel said, already holding a roll of tape like a weapon. Darling, this is the Olympics of gift wrapping, and we are the dream team."

"Dream team?" Donovan appeared beside Marcel. "I thought we were just here to wrap gifts, I didn't know we were starting a league."

"Yes, my guy, we are definitely in a league of our own." Marcel replied. "Shall we get started? I think Donovan and I will grab the gifts and bring them over to you two."

Clapping her hands Katy said, "Yes, the ones with the muscles, you'll grab gifts and bring them over. Eden, be careful. Don't let Donovan hog all the tape. That's a rookie mistake."

Eden felt her lips twitch into a smile. "Now, this is going to be interesting."

"Interesting? Donovan said with a raised eyebrow. "I think you mean chaotic and tad bit humiliating."

Eden laughed saying, "Okay fine. Yeah, that too."

Unrolling a massive sheet of wrapping paper, Marcel said leaning over to Donovan, "Keep an eye on Eden. She's dangerous when she gets competitive."

"Competitive huh?" Donovan echoed, watching Eden carefully as she began inspecting her first gift, a plush teddy bear looking far too small for the mountain of paper beside it.

"Oh absolutely," Marcel whispered back grinning. "She's got that laser focus. You better watch out for your ankles."

Busy wrapping the bear, trying to make the folds perfect, Eden didn't hear the conversation. The tape seemed to have a mind of its own. Her first attempt resulted in a crumpled mess. She looked up to find Donovan standing beside her, offering a steady hand.

"Need some help?" he asked.

"Maybe. It depends, how good are you at this?" Eden said, with a playful edge to her voice.

"I've wrapped a few things in my life. Mostly files, but close enough, right?"

Eden laughed and for a moment, the chaos around them, the toys, the rolls of ribbon, Katy yelling at a misbehaving tape dispenser, all faded into the background.

Katy's voice cut through the air. "Eden! Over here! We've got a line forming! The North Pole is waiting!"

Eden and Donovan followed to Katy's table. Surrounded by small crowds of volunteers from various other companies, all trying to keep up. Marcel and Donovan set up a station to ensure efficiency and holiday magic.

Donovan was calm and measured. While Marcel was loudly narrating his own technique.

"Step one," Marcel said dramatically, holding up a roll of wrapping paper like a sword. "Precision. Step two, fold like your life depends on it. Step three...flourish!"

"Flourish, man?" Donovan asked.

"Yes, flourish! Did I stutter? Watch and learn," Marcel said, executing a wildly unnecessary paper twirl, which ended with a slapstick crash as the tape dispenser flew across the table.

Everyone laughed, even Donovan, who rarely lost his composure did in that moment.

Leaning in, whispering conspiratorially, Katy said, "See? Told you this would be fun. Or at least, funny!"

By the time the first mountain of gifts were wrapped, the *dream team* had developed their own rhythm. Eden, Katy, Marcel, and Donovan unintentionally created a cadence, fold, tape, laugh, repeat. The rip of the paper and the snap of tape helped them keep the time.

Volunteers from other companies were cheering each other on, while some were deliberately sabotaging each other with misplaced tape and scissors, and others offered encouragement.

At one point, Donovan tried demonstrating his folding technique to Eden. "See? You want the crease, crisp! Like this." He said folding his paper expertly.

"It looks exactly like how I do it. Only, you know, mine with slightly more flair." Eden replied.

"Flair is definitely mandatory." Donovan said with a wink.

Marcel, slipped in right behind Katy kissed her on the cheek from behind and whispered, "They're...undeniable."

"I know. Shh, let's see how long it takes them to notice we're watching."

They never noticed. Nor did they notice others watching as well.

By the end of their shift, their laughter had echoed throughout the warehouse as they'd wrapped hundreds of gifts.

In their time together, they all walked away with a sense of the joy of giving, the pure delight in service, and how it could be amplified when shared with others.

Cleaning up their stations, one of the foundation's founders approached, "You four were incredible. You have the energy, the heart, and clearly the chemistry we've been looking for. Our original hosts had to cancel. We'd love to ask you all to host and MC the actual event on Friday. What do you say?"

They exchanged glances with each other searching for agreement.

"We'd love to," they all said in unison.

"Yes!" Katy squealed, punching the air." I knew this was going to be fun. Maybe we are the real deal *dream team*."

Later at home, Eden retrieved her gratitude set from earlier in the day. She still needed to complete her assignment. With her fingers wrapped around the gratitude pen, she easily completed the remaining items she was grateful for.

Gratitude wasn't just a list of fifty things. It was the space she was creating to notice. To participate and allow joy to take root deep down inside.

Joy was returning and gratitude had made room for it to stay.

Chapter 16

Thursday arrived with a hush, like the world was holding something back on purpose.

The big foundation's event was tomorrow. Friday had weight now. Friday night now came with lights, laughter, microphones, and people. But today wasn't asking for performance. Today, was asking for attention.

Stepping into her office, Eden paused.

Front and center on her desk sat a tall, carefully wrapped box. There was no card attached at the top this time. Just presence.

Closing the door behind her, she let out a small laugh. "Alright," she said softly. "I see you."

Inside the box was a mirror. Not just any mirror but the kind that belonged on a vanity or an altar. Framed in warm gold and etched with delicate detail.

Beneath it lay a folded card.

Day 9: Return to Wonder. *What is trying to be revealed in you in this season*? **Write three sentences beginning with: I forgot that...**

Leaning the mirror against the desk, Eden took a stalled moment and looked at her reflection. Not the quick check kind of looking. Not the critique kind either.

The noticing kind.

Tilting her head, she studied the woman staring back at her. The softer eyes. The steadied shoulders. The smile that came across more easily than it used to.

With all the assignments she'd been having over the last week and a half, she'd designated her trusted planner as the safe space for these assignments.

Reaching for it from her bag, she decided to write the first sentence without thinking too hard.

I forgot that joy doesn't need permission.

Closing her portfolio, she thought, not because she was done but because she wasn't meant to rush this.

If that realization didn't interrupt her, the mere mayhem outside her door would have.

Peering around the frame of her door, looking down the hallway, a winter wonderland on a caffeine high had been born. Garland draped over door frames. Fake snow clung to cubicle walls and someone had gone rogue with the tinsel.

And then there was Katy.

"Eden!" Katy called, popping up from her behind a six-foot inflatable snowman that one hundred percent did not belong in a professional environment. "I need your opinion. Should we go classy winter lodge or full-on North Pole Madness?"

"We? When did you start speaking French Katy?"

"Yes, *we Mademoiselle*," Katy said, already taping something glittery to Eden's office door. "Since your door has the best lighting, you are my dear, my, I mean, our best chance at winning."

"You really stay trying to win something Katy," Eden said laughing.

"Only the office decoration competition," Katy said, like it was obvious. "I have been preparing for this moment since last Christmas when accounting beat us with their lazy, minimalist snowflake theme. And, since they upped the ante with the prize money!"

"You do realize I haven't consented to your game plan to overthrow accounting...or anyone else competing today."

"You consented when you walked into the building," Katy replied cheerfully. "Now, hold this," handing Eden a string of lights.

Eden could feel the lightness. The ridiculousness. The wonder sneaking in through tinsel and merriment.

"I forgot that play can be productive," she thought.

She didn't write this one down, but she did let it saturate and marinate her spirit.

With their winning display of a combined theme, classy winter lodge and maddening North Pole all complete, lunchtime was striking everyone's stomachs.

Amara, right on time, appeared at Eden's door carrying two bags and wearing her familiar smile of knowing.

"There you are," Amara said. "I feel like I haven't seen you in forever. Feels like I've been gone for a year."

"It does feel like you've been gone for a minute. So much has happened," Eden said, standing to hug her. "We have a lot to catch up on. How was your trip with Grant?"

"It was great. Even though it was one of his work trips, he was intentional about scheduling time for us to enjoy and have a good time. And boy did we have a good time. But enough about me. I want to know what's been going on with you. Cause, I see something."

"You see what?" Eden said laughing.

"Go on and fill me in Girl. Tell me what's been going on." Amara nodded slowly with warm eyes.

Settling in and spreading lunch across Eden's desk. Amara listened as Eden filled her in on all the recent highlights in her life. The highlight reel included the most recent letters and assignments. The unexpected joy of gift wrapping. Being asked to host the event.

"Hmm, there's something different about you," she said. "It's like you're inspiring me without even trying."

"Aww, that might be one of the nicest things anyone's ever said to me." Eden replied.

"It's true though. But who do you think is sending you these gifts and assignments? Do you have a secret admirer or something?" Amara asked.

"At this point, I don't know and I don't care. In the beginning, I was trying to figure out but now I'm like, it really doesn't matter. I'm enjoying the process." Eden said smiling.

"Sooo, is Christopher your date for tomorrow evening, to see you shine like the Christmas lights as a host?"

Pausing before she answered, Eden replied. "He said he was going to come since he wasn't able to make the gift wrapping. He's just so super-duper busy with work."

"Aren't we all." Amara quipped. Then, casually, she asked, "Well, what are you wearing?"

"I haven't decided yet?"

Raising her eyebrow, Amara said, "You're hosting an event tomorrow. With a microphone. In front of people. The girl who's been praying for people to see her. Is now going to be seen and she doesn't know what she's going to wear?"

"I know."

"And yet you haven't decided. It looks like I came home right in time."

"I mean, there's nothing for you to worry about. Trust. I have options." Eden said confidently.

"Well good, I'm glad to hear that. Just make sure it isn't made of armor. You have a tendency to try and hide. I hope your options include you wearing something that lets you be seen.

Exhaling, Eden took out her pen and planner and wrote, *I forgot that I don't need to hide to be safe.*

"I just thought about something. Are you and Grant available tomorrow evening? Do you want to come to the event?"

"Um ma'am, I was already planning to come when you first said it. You didn't even have to ask that question. Yes, we'll be there. On that note, I'm going to get out of here. I'll check in with you later."

Amara left Eden with nothing but more thoughts. Looking in the mirror again, she picked up her pen and wrote the third sentence.

I forgot that I'm allowed to enjoy this season as its unfolding.

Closing the planner, something was awakened.

It felt like trust.

Today had done its work and the joy and wonder of the days unfolding felt like something beautiful standing just out of view.

Chapter 17

F riday wasn't taking any chances easing in. It'd arrived fully
dressed.

"Hey Katy, can you come into my office for a minute?" Eden beckoned.

Entering Eden's office, Katy replied, "Hey, what's up? Everything
okay?"

Katy was late to work that morning, so she hadn't had an opportunity to place Eden's gift for day ten yet.

"Everything is fine. I just wanted to let you know, I'm only working
a half day today. I have some errands to run before this evening's event,
so I'll be leaving shortly."

Trying to figure out how she could place the gift before Eden left
Katy said, "Umm, okay. I'll probably end up doing the same."

"Um Katy, didn't you come in late this morning?"

"Yes. Yes, I did. But you know, it's the holidays. Is anybody really
working these days?"

"I am!" Eden exclaimed.

"Well, maybe you shouldn't be. In fact, do you want to go downstairs and grab a latte?" Katy offered. "My treat. You know you can't pass up those lattes from downstairs."

Without thinking twice, Eden popped up from her desk and said, "You know what? Why not. Let's go. Especially if you're treating."

Eden and Katy started making their way downstairs when Katy pretended to leave her wallet at her desk.

"You go ahead and I'll catch up with you. I'll be right back." Katy instructed.

As Eden took the elevator down alone, Katy dashed back to place the day's gift and assignment.

Upon their return with lattes in hand, Eden walked in to find a small brass compass inside a velvet pouch on her desk.

Looking back at Katy, Eden asked. "When you came back up here, did you do this? Did you see who did this?"

Looking unaware, Katy said, "Uh, I can't really say."

That response was perfect because she really couldn't say or she would bust her cover.

The compass was solid and cool to touch. It was the kind that belonged to explorers and leaders, not wanderers. The card beneath it read:

Day 10: Return to Purpose. Direction matters more than speed. Write one sentence that will guide the next decade of your life.

"This is just...I don't know what to say." Eden said turning the compass slowly in the palm of her hand. "I still don't know how these gifts are getting here," she added, quieter now. "But this...this feels intentional."

Offering a shrug, a shrug far too casual for the moment, Katy said, "I've said it before, just enjoy it. You don't need to solve everything."

"I guess you're right," Eden said. "That's what I've been doing." Eden replied.

"And it's been great right?"

Eden's phone buzzed before she could respond. Christopher was calling.

Eden answered the phone nearly singing the word, "Hi!"

Hearing Eden's cheerful disposition crushed Christopher internally.

"I hate this," he said, exhaling.

"You hate my singing? All I said was hi." Eden said jokingly.

"No, no, no. I'm sorry. It has nothing to do with your singing and everything to do with what I'm about to tell you." Christopher shared.

"Why does this sound serious? Is everything okay Christopher?"

Frustration sailed out of his mouth even through a steady tone, he said, "I just got pulled into something I can't get out of. I'm not going to be able to make it tonight, even though I said I was."

"I understand," Eden said. And she did.

"Are you open to meeting up at the coffee shop we met up at last week in the morning? We could try matcha together." He suggested.

Smiling softly, she said, "Yes, that'll be fine. I can meet you."

Eden and Christopher ended the call with warmth intact. No tension. No disappointment. Just timing being honest.

Chapter 18

The foundation's holiday event unfolded like something that had been waiting for the right people to steward it. Strings of warm lights framed the entrance. Tables overflowed with wrapped gifts, their ribbons catching the glow like sparkling lights. Children's laughter echoed from one end of the space while volunteers darted back and forth with clipboards and walkie-talkies.

The community center was buzzing. The DJ, off in the distance, tested the microphone with an enthusiastic, "Mic check, mic check, ho ho ho!"

Standing off stage, Eden smoothed her bold and celebratory amethyst colored dress, heart steady but alert. The kind of alertness that comes when you know you're about to be useful in a way that matters.

"You look beautiful. Are you ready for tonight?" Donovan asked quietly beside her.

Nodding she said, "I think so. If I forget my name, just point at me and smile."

"I can do that, he said smiling. "I can definitely smile at you, he said smiling. "And names are optional."

Katy leaned across the two of them, whisper-shouting, "Okay but if either of you freeze, Marcel and I will start singing a Christmas song."

Marcel adjusted his jacket. "Oh no we won't. Speak for yourself. I can't sing a lick."

All four of them let out a huge laugh. Enough to calm any last-minute jitters.

"Places everyone!" A volunteer called.

The curtains opened. Eden adjusted her microphone once, glanced at Marcel and Katy, and exchanged a look with Donovan that didn't need words. They were all in sync. Not rehearsed but aligned.

From the moment they welcomed the crowd, it was clear. They worked.

"Good evening everyone and welcome to the holiday toy giveaway," Eden said smiling out over the crowd. "If you're for joy and generosity, and a *little* holiday mischief..."

"You're in the right place," Donovan finished smoothly.

The crowd responded with laughter.

Stepping forward, Marcel said, "So let's give it up for our volunteers because without them, this would just be four random people up here with no toys."

"Which we'd still be a whole vibe, by the way." Katy added.

Laughter rippled through the center.

Marcel brought the charisma. Katy brought the sparkle and perfectly timed humor. Donovan grounded the room with his calm authority.

And Eden? Eden held the space. She bridged joy and gravity effortlessly, speaking with warmth that didn't ask for permission.

The crowd leaned in whenever she spoke.

Across the room, Amara watched with folded arms and a knowing smile.

"Oh," she whispered. "I see what's happening here."

Grant followed her eyes and nodded once. Noticing Eden's ease, he also observed Donovan's attentiveness, and how people were naturally gravitating towards them.

As the evening unfolded, Eden watched the impact happen in real time.

Kids clutching gifts like buried treasures.

Parents exhaling relief.

Community leaders exchanging looks that said, *This is great work.*

The quartet hosting called for a brief intermission.

The excitement and exhilaration of the first set had them feeling amazing.

Marcel loved being there and it showed. The kids flocked to him as he walked through the center.

Donovan leaned in close to Eden and said, "You see that family over there?"

"The one with the twins?" Eden asked.

"Yeah. Their block is part of the revitalization corridor."

Eden's breath caught slightly. "You're kidding."

"No, I'm not. This is policy work, he said gently. "With a human touch. I'm glad they were able to at least get something, but I feel bad the older kids aren't really represented here. There are a lot of toys but what about the older kids?"

Listening to Donovan, something in Eden's chest shifted. It felt like purpose brushing up against practice.

"Would you like anything to drink before we go into the next set?" Donovan asked.

"You know...I think I would like some water." Eden replied.

Nearing the refreshment table, Donovan saw Marcel and Katy talking, only they didn't see him.

Katy, laughing too loudly, with Marcel gesturing animatedly discussing their master plan to connect Eden and Donovan with the gifts. The details of their plan drifted right across Donovan's ears.

Unaware of his presence. Donovan stood behind them until they had no choice but to feel his presence.

"So," he said, hands in his pocket. "You two want to tell me how long you've been masquerading as Cupid dressed as elves?

Marcel winced. Katy froze.

"Oh," Katy said finally. "You weren't supposed to hear that."

"Oh really? Well, how was I supposed to find out?" Hold on. So let me get this straight," he said. "You two have been running a full-blown holiday transformation operation...under the guise it was me doing this for Eden?"

"In our defense," Marcel said, "it was for love. It sounded better at the time."

Exhaling, Donovan shook his head. "You know, I wondered."

"Wondered what?" Katy asked.

"I had a feeling something was up the other day but I didn't say anything. So, fill me in on all the details of this operation and don't leave out a single detail."

Katy and Marcel relayed all of their battle plans to Donovan.

"Are you mad at us?" Katy asked.

"Mad? No way. I appreciate what you were trying to do," he said. "Truly. But I'll take it from here. If gifts are being sent to Eden from me, from here on out...they'll actually be coming from me."

"Respect and fair enough." Marcel said studying him for a beat, then nodded.

"And if you need any help with logistics, we'll help." Katy said exhaling.

"You've done enough but I'll let you know." Donovan said.

And just like that, the baton was passed.

"I was starting to think you forgot about me." Eden teased as Donovan joined her again with a bottle of water.

"Not even close." Donovan said. "Are you ready to close this thing out?"

"Yes, I am. Let's do it."

The show closed to applause, gratitude, and a line of people wanting to know Eden's name, her role, and where she'd been hiding.

She answered politely. Briefly. Letting the moment speak for itself.

As the crowd thinned and volunteers began the cleanup, Donovan approached Eden.

"Walk with me?" he asked.

Stepping aside, the noise softened behind them.

"You were incredible tonight." He said.

"So were you. Oh my goodness, that was so much fun. I had a great time." She replied.

Hesitating only for a second, he asked, "I would love to continue this great time. Would you allow me to take you out? Dinner. Just us, tomorrow night?"

Eden looked at Donovan. Really looked at him.

"Yes," she said smiling. "I'd love that."

"Wonderful. I'll call you tomorrow. I loved serving with you tonight, Eden." Donovan said moving in for a good night hug.

"Likewise." She said.

Later that night, alone at home. Eden finally sat down to write out her purpose statement. Placing the compass on the table, allowing it to anchor the moment, she wrote:

My purpose for the next decade is to build what lasts: love, community, and spaces where people are seen, starting with my own life.

Chapter 19

"So," Christopher said, leaning in to greet Eden, "you decided to return to the scene of the crime."

"I mean, what can I say the matcha lattes here are worth committing a crime over." Eden replied jokingly.

Bean There, Filed That was already alive when Eden arrived. Steam curled from mugs; low Christmas music hummed beneath mumbled conversations. It was a place that held many versions of her and asked for nothing in return.

"I was waiting for you before I ordered so you could instruct me on how to order this crime worthy matcha." Christopher said.

They ordered, found seating that would allow them a semi-private conversation, and for a few moments simply existed in the quiet comfort they'd built. Two people who genuinely enjoy each other's company.

"What a week huh? I haven't seen you since our date here last week. Where you shared with me your devotional from that morning that, honestly, encouraged me throughout the week." Christopher admitted.

Eden smiled to herself. He remembered.

Christopher continued, quietly reciting. "...and I pray that Christ will make his home in your hearts through faith. I pray that you may have your roots and foundations in love."[1]

"Oh my goodness Christopher, you remembered."

Looking deeply at Eden, Christopher replied, "I don't forget things that matter."

Christopher's name was called, and he left to grab their order.

Settling into her seat, Eden sat thinking of a strong reply.

When he returned, Christopher was the first to speak.

"Cheers," he said having his first taste of Eden's favorite drink. "Oh wow, I see why you came back here. I didn't think I was going to like this but surprisingly I do."

Sharing a laugh, they do a little more chit-chatting, but Christopher turned somewhat serious.

Reaching for her hand, he said, "I want to tell you something."

Eden nodded. "Okay."

"I don't talk about this much now," he continued. "But before I had this job, before everything you now know about my life, I was a professional athlete.

Tilting her head slightly, she said, "Oh, I wasn't aware of that."

"Nowadays, most people aren't. It's not something I lead with." He smiled, faint but real. "I got injured. It was career-ending. And it was...let's just say, an adjustment."

He explained his truth in a way that didn't hold bitterness or any drama, but it was his truth.

"This job," he said gesturing vaguely, "keeps me connected to the world of sports that I love. In a way, it's like a second chance. And one I don't take lightly."

Eden listened with presence.

"And because of that," he continued, "it requires a lot of me. More than I sometimes want to admit."

Eden was sensing his uneasiness. She sat and let him finish without interruption.

Brushing his thumbs against her hand, he looked down and then up at her. "Eden, I really like you. I like your mind, your warmth, the way you light up when you talk about *your* work."

"We do both like to work a lot. And I can tell your work is important to you and I like that about you as well." She said.

They shared mutual admiration for each other.

Christopher looked up at Eden with soft eyes.

"I meditated on that devotional a lot this week and after I wasn't able to make the holiday event where you were the host. I knew this was the right thing to do."

Internally, Eden braced herself for what she sensed was coming.

"Right now, my life is full," he said gently. "So full I'm unintentionally asking you to wait for me in the margins. And that doesn't feel right. Especially not at Christmas time and with your birthday coming up."

His voice lowered.

"This season is about making room. And, I apparently don't have it yet, like I thought I did. It feels like we're the victims of bad timing."

Silence settled between them. It wasn't heavy, it was sacred.

He took one of his hands and rubbed it along his jawline, exhaling slowly, like he'd been carrying these words all morning.

"I keep cancelling on you," he said grabbing her hand again. "I don't want to be the kind of man who asks for patience and understanding when what I really don't have is space. Love, it needs somewhere to live. I don't want to dishonor what could potentially be a great love story by rushing it into a life that can't hold it."

Eden felt something rise up on the inside of her. It wasn't sadness. It wasn't disappointment.

It was relief and respect.

"Thank you," she said softly. "For telling me this and for being honest."

"I didn't want to waste your time," he said. "Or dull something that feels...important."

"I really appreciate that, Christopher. I really do. It's been great getting to know you."

"Eden, I want you to know, you are an incredible woman. I want you to know, I'm not walking away because I don't care," he said. I'm stepping back, because I do. Give me six months to settle some of these obligations and I'm going to do this, the right way."

Squeezing her hand just a little tighter and for another moment he blessed her.

"I hope," he said softly, "that when love shows up for you, it has all the space it needs."

She smiled, eyes sweetly. "I hope the same for you."

When they hugged goodbye, it wasn't complicated. It was clean. They both walked away with the understanding, some endings don't feel like loss. They could just be on hiatus.

[1] *Ephesians 3:17 Good News Translation*

Chapter 20

Saturday evening arrived soft, like it had nothing to prove.

Donovan chose a restaurant that reflected exactly that. Warm lighting. Wood tables worn smooth by years of conversations. A place where people came to talk, not perform. It was the kind of restaurant where time slowed if you let it.

Eden noticed, as she always did, that he stood when she approached. In his hand was a bouquet of flowers, thoughtful and unmistakably intentional.

"You didn't have to do that," she said, smiling.

"I know," he replied easily, pulling out her chair. "I wanted to. Hello there beautiful. These are for you."

"Thank you so much, she said, genuinely touched. "They're lovely."

As she sat, something quietly clicked into place. The difference between obligation and choice has been revealing itself more clearly these days. And Donovan, was a chooser.

They ordered dinner and quickly found themselves recapping the foundation's toy drive, slipping into the conversation with familiarity that surprised Eden. Their shared concern naturally returned to the same place.

"It really bothered me, you know," he said, stirring his drink slowly. "Seeing all that joy but also seeing who didn't quite get reached."

"Yeah, the twelve-and-up kids," Eden acknowledged. "There's a quiet gap there."

Meeting her eyes, Donovan said, "What if next year, we close it? What if we close that gap?"

"There's that we word again," she thought.

Eden didn't react outwardly, but something was happening internally.

"We could," she said carefully. We could do a gift card drive. From what I could tell, toys will always show up for the little ones, but the older kids get overlooked. Doing a gift card drive could help close that gap."

"That's exactly what I was thinking." He said.

Then, with intent, Donovan reached into the inside pocket of his jacket.

"I have something I want to give to you tonight. I have a little gift for you."

"Oh, Donovan," she laughed lightly. "You didn't have to get me anything."

"I know," he said again. "But I wanted to. But I need to explain something first.

Eden looked up at Donovan with curiosity flickering in her eyes.

Taking in a deep breath, Donovan said, "Katy and Marcel," he began. "Yeah, those two. I believe their hearts were in the right place.

Um, I know about the gifts. I know about the notes, the assignments, they told me everything."

"They told you what?" Eden asked.

"Katy explained to me she's been sending you these gifts lately with the hopes you'd think they were coming from me."

"She did *what*?!" Eden exclaimed. "I'm going to kill her!" Fire erupted inside of her, and it wasn't a menopausal hot flash.

"Easy," he said quickly, holding up his hand. "No violence at Christmas. And truth be told, they didn't ruin anything. She and Marcel were doing exactly what they were meant to do. Look at it like this, they were midwives, they were never to be owners of this operation."

Eden leaned back processing. Then realization smacked her in the face.

Thinking back over the last several days when the gifts started arriving.

"I *knew* it, she said suddenly. "Well...I didn't know, but I did."

Donovan laughed.

"You're adorable." He said.

Eden sat trying to piece together the last couple of weeks.

"Once I found out," he said, sliding a small box onto the table in her direction, "I told them I'd take it from here. Fully. It wasn't meant to stay anonymous."

He didn't push the box, he simply let it rest between them, like an offering.

Choosing his words carefully, he said, "I'm calling it your very own Jubilee Advent Calendar of sorts."

Eden's lips parted in surprise.

"Each day," he said, "isn't about counting down to your birthday. It is about making room."

Eden placed her hand across her heart.

And today's theme is Renew Imagination.

Eden finally opened the box.

Inside rested a vintage looking key. It was decorative and substantial, looking like it carried decades of history.

Donovan watched Eden closely. Not for approval, but for understanding.

"Eden, this isn't a key for effort," he said gently. "It's a key for access. With a Jubilee birthday, jubilee isn't about forcing doors to open. It is about noticing which ones are already unlocked."

Eden's fingers curled around the key instinctively.

"And whenever fear tells you to be practical too early," he continued, "touch the key. Remember this. Imagination isn't about fantasy. It's the language God uses before He builds."

Eden exhaled slowly, "Wow, I love that, Donovan."

He had a way of calming her down without trying to.

Beneath the key sat a small card.

Day 11: Renew Imagination. Take 30 minutes. No edits. No fixing. Finish the sentences: It's a random Tuesday and I'm ... and I wake up excited because.... Circle anything that makes you smile.

Eden didn't say anything right away. She didn't need to.

"Thank you," she finally whispered.

They sat still, allowing the moment to breathe.

Her phone buzzed.

Then his.

They looked down at the same time.

Board nominations for the both of them.

Eden laughed first. A real one. The kind that surprises itself.

"Well," she said, shaking her head. "I didn't see that coming. Did you?"

Donovan smiled. "I'm not surprised. You were dynamite up there. This is your visibility test."

"But I wasn't up there by myself." She countered.

"Well," he said lightly, "then they must've felt sorry for me and my ugly face."

"Oh, stop," she laughed. Don't ever say that again."

Dessert arrived and Donovan cleared his throat.

"My family's getting together tomorrow night," he said casually, like it wasn't a big deal even though it was. "With Hannukah starting tomorrow. We kick off what we call Love and Light week."

"Mmm, that already sounds like a brand." Eden teased.

Laughing, Donovan said, "The opener is our annual Mingle Jingle. Or Merrykkah. It all depends on who's naming this year. It's a combined Christmas and Hanukkah family gathering."

Intrigued, Eden turned her head, "Hmm, tell me more."

"My family's interfaith," he explained. "Jewish and Christian roots all mashed up together in there. Growing up, I didn't fully understand it but now I see how much it shaped me." He paused. "I'd love for you to join us."

Without hesitation, Eden quickly said, "I'd love that and thank you for inviting me."

Something unspoken passed between them.

"Just so you know," Donovan added with a grin, "now that I've taken over the gifts brigade, I'm going to have to find reasons to see you."

Eden opened her mouth to respond but the words tangled somewhere between hope and surprise.

"I ...."

He laughed gently and rescued her. "Switching gears. Someone has a birthday coming up. Any plans yet?"

She deflected, as she always did when that question came up.

"Nope, not yet."

He didn't press. He simply noticed.

As they stood to leave, Eden slipped the key into her coat pocket. It rested there like a new promise.

For the first time in a long time, she wasn't bracing for disappointment. She wasn't waiting for the other shoe to drop.

She was making space for all the good, life was ready to bring and unlock within her.

Chapter 21

The morning arrived without an agenda. No alarms. No rushing. No performance. Just light filtering in slowly, like it had
manners.

The city outside was awake but unbothered. Even the traffic seemed
to understand it was Sunday.

Eden reached for the letter on her nightstand.

Her godfather's letter.

She'd read it before. More than once. It had quietly become her
morning devotional. Today, she read it differently, slower. As if the
words aged overnight and gained new meaning.

I've seen you carry your burdens with grace beyond your own beliefs.

Eden exhaled, as if letting the weight of it all pass through her.

That line landed somewhere deeper than thought. It landed in
memory.

She carried the letter with her to the living room, wrapped herself
in a blanket, and sat near the window.

Her eyes drifted to her planner, still open to the previous day's assignment.

Renew Imagination.

Eden picked up the key Donovan had given her, resting beside her planner and rolled it between her fingers. It felt solid, like something meant to last.

She reread what she'd written the night before after her date with Donovan.

It's a random Tuesday and I'm laughing on my way to work.
I wake up excited because my life feels abundantly fulfilled.

Her phone buzzed on the coffee table. Katy's face and name flashed across the screen.

Then again.

And again.

Eden chose not to answer. Not out of avoidance but out of discernment. She was still absorbing what Katy had done. This morning was not meant for explaining but for listening.

"We'll talk tomorrow, Katy." She said to the phone.

Her phone buzzed again, this time with a different name.

She smiled and answered.

"Good morning doll," Liora said with her voice warm and unhurried. "I was thinking about you. What's going on in your world?"

"Funny you should say that," Eden replied. "I was doing the same."

They talked easily at first. About nothing important. And then gently, about everything.

Eden told her mother each story in detail.

The gifts.

Christopher.

Katy and Marcel.

Donovan.

The toy drive.

The board nomination.

The Mingle Jingle.

Liora listened without interrupting.

Finally, she said, "You are entitled to feel how you feel. But this all sounds like wonderful news to me."

"Mama, you would say that. But it's...a lot! I just wonder sometimes if all this, and especially Donovan, is too good to be true? He's like a unicorn."

Liora chuckled, "That is how you know it's real my dear. Trust where this road is leading you. You are a blessed individual, and good things are heading your way."

"Thank you, Mama."

"Listen, you have always known how to hear life when it's speaking. Make sure you are leaning in and listening right now."

"Yeah," Eden said lifting her chin and shoulders, "I'm going to take the rest of the morning and do just that...listen. I think I'm going to take a nap and then get ready to meet Donovan at his parent's house."

"You'll have to call me tomorrow and let me know how everything went. I've never heard of a Merrykah." Liora said laughing.

"Neither have I which is why I wanted to attend." Eden said.

Liora shifted from their casual conversation to a pointed question. "Are you sure that's why you wanted to attend?" She said with a smirk. "If this Donovan is as fine and thoughtful as you say he is. I think that's the real reason you're going."

Answering with a small nod and slowed words, Eden replied, "That could be part of it too."

As her mother always did, she ended the conversation before Eden could.

"Tonight, when you go over to his family, this isn't about you needing to be impressive. Show up as Eden. This season is asking you to listen. Don't rush past that. I love you and I'll talk to you tomorrow."

After they hung up, Eden prepared a cup of hot tea and settled onto the sofa, where sleep came easily.

Outside, the afternoon light dimmed.

And somewhere across town, love was preparing a table.

Chapter 22

The Rivera house announced itself before Eden ever stepped inside.

Laughter spilled out first. Then music. Then the unmistakable sound of a child yelling someone's name with zero regard for volume or timing.

"You made it," Donovan said with genuine relief in his voice, as if the evening couldn't fully begin until she arrived.

As the door swung open, warmth rushed out.

"Is she here?" A voice called from somewhere deep inside the house.

Eden barely had time to take in the scene before someone handed her a drink, someone took her coat, and a small child stared at her shoes like they were a personal invitation.

"Who's this?" the child asked as another child darted past her legs.

"This is Eden," Donovan said smiling.

"Oh. Hi Eden, bye Eden," the child said and ran away.

The living room housed a mixture of furniture that looked collected over decades, not coordinated. Family photos lined the walls. No staged portraits, they were more like, moments. Someone mid-laugh. Someone squinting in the sun. A child asleep on a shoulder.

"This is...lively," Eden said, leaning in toward Donovan.

"Oh, this is calm. Give it about another hour," he said.

The house moved like a living thing. People crossing paths, doubling back, speaking over one another, kissing cheeks. There was no central host because everyone seemed to be hosting.

A candelabra for menorah sat proudly on the mantel, candles waiting. A Christmas tree glowed nearby, its ornaments mismatched and meaningful.

Holiday greetings filled the house, written in both Hebrew and English. *Chag Sameach, Chag Urim Sameach*, alongside *Merry Christmas* and *Happy Holidays*.

Somewhere in the kitchen, someone was arguing about cinnamon. There were stories being shared, some, dating back over generations.

"I'm glad you're here. We need another adult who can referee." Someone said.

Shrugging her shoulders, Eden laughed, "I don't know the rules."

"Perfect," the woman replied. "Neither do we."

As they moved through the home, Donovan introduced Eden to his immediate family, his parents and siblings who all lovingly welcomed her with open arms. They welcomed Eden into their home and their hearts.

In the kitchen, two women worked side by side, one flipping latkes, the other making sweet potato pies. A brisket sat resting on the counter beside a honey-glazed ham. Someone announced there was baked macaroni and cheese, to which everyone cheered. Music played softly, shifting between familiar holiday classics and Christmas soul.

"Food diplomacy," Donovan shared beside her.

"I like it," Eden said. "Very effective."

When it came time to light the menorah, the room gathered without being summoned. A hush fell over the room as conversations paused naturally in reverence.

The blessing was spoken clearly, lovingly, and without performance. Eden didn't understand every word but she understood the tone.

Afterward, Christmas music crept back in. A game broke out, involving a version of charades with very few rules. Eden found herself laughing harder than she had in weeks as someone dramatically failed to act out, "Silent Night."

The little kids were dancing like there was a competition no one had announced.

Eden stood back for a moment, unnoticed, and how rare it felt. To be present without being managed. To be welcomed without being evaluated.

"Hey," Donovan said, appearing beside her. "Come with me for a second."

Leading her by the hand, he took her to a quieter corner of the house, near a small table by the window.

"I have something for you," he said. Opening the closet by the table he pulled out a tiny gift bag.

"You don't have to open this now," he said. "I just wanted to give it to you before it got really crazy in here. This is for when things get quiet again. You'll understand it later."

A knock and a wave on the window from outside made Donovan smile.

Seconds later, the front door opened.

Inside the room where Eden and Donovan were a young woman stood a few feet away, watching them with a confident smile.

"Dad," the young woman said, her voice airy and bright.

"Hey!" Donovan said, pulling her into a hug that was familiar and full.

Eden noticed how his shoulders became softer.

"This is my daughter, Krista," he said to Eden, like it was the most natural thing in the world.

Eden smiled, extending her hand. "It's so nice to meet you."

"Likewise. I've heard good things."

No need to ask from who.

As they rejoined the group, someone was passing out small gifts to the kids.

Another group was playing in the traditional Rivera dreidel tournament. A time-honored family tradition that held serious bragging rights for the entire year. The brackets were stacked well for intense competition.

Eden sat on the floor with kids who insisted she join them to play with them and their new gifts. A child leaning against her made perfect sense.

When Eden decided it was time to leave, someone gathered her belongings with commentary and the hugs were plentiful. Eden was leaving with more than just the gift Donovan had given her; she was leaving with so many others.

"I'm glad you came," he said.

"So am I," she replied. "I had a great time with you and your family tonight."

Love and Light week had begun. The mingling and the jingling was a huge success and Eden was no longer a stranger to Merrykah.

"Call me when you get home," Donovan said whispering in her ear as he hugged her goodbye.

"I will. Thanks again for my gift and a lovely evening."

Back inside her home, Eden opened her gifts, she started with the gifts from Donovan's family. All nice little trinkets but she was grateful they thought of her.

She saved Donovan's gift for last.

Inside the gift bag was a smooth, small stone and a note card: **Day 12: Blessing your past. Think and thank. Think about every version of you that got you to this point. The versions who knew better. And the versions who didn't. Stones endure, they remember and this is something to hold onto when remembering gets complicated.**

Eden read the card and examined the finish on the stone. She closed her fingers around it.

Her throat tightened but she smiled.

The stone rested in her hand, but Donovan was beginning to settle into her heart.

Chapter 23

Entering the office building, the usual crowds were light. It was clear people were taking their paid time off and already easing into Christmas vacation.

The morning didn't rush Eden and that alone felt strange. It was as if nothing sacred had happened over the weekend.

Even without the usual bustle, the office lights still hummed on schedule and emails waited patiently, pretending they hadn't been offended by two days of silence.

Eden noticed, though, *she* felt different moving through it all.

Katy's desk was empty. She hadn't arrived yet. Fear had a way of making people late. Or quiet. Or careful.

Eden entered her office and sat her bag down and settled into her chair. She rolled her shoulders back once and took in breath before logging in. It was small, the kind of pause she used to skip. Her body seemed to appreciate being consulted.

Within five minutes, her phone rang.

"Tell me everything," Amara said without a preamble. "From the moment you arrived, to the moment you left."

"Well good morning to you too." Eden replied.

"You told me you were going to call me last night after you got home and you didn't, so let's skip all of the pleasantries. I'm nosy, I want details, what happened?"

Eden smiled, rolling her neck slowly. "You want to know what happened with what?"

"Girl don't play with me. You know what I'm calling about. And I don't want the highlight reel. I want the whole shebang."

"It was...full," she said finally. It was loud. Warm. Unexpected."

"Those are three words you don't usually put together," Amara said.

"I know."

They both paused, a pause that invited more without demanding it.

"The family gathering was interfaith, his father is Jewish, and his mother is Christian," Eden added. "From the oldest to the youngest, there were multiple generations represented. Kids were running everywhere. The food was everything and there was zero control in the entire home."

"And?" Amara prompted.

"And I didn't feel like I needed any."

"Oh my God," Amara laughed. "We're about to have us a shabach and a shalom romance up in here. I want an invite to Merrykah next year. I need to learn how to play dreidel."

Eden laughed, full and unrestrained, the kind of laughter that surprised even her.

They talked for a few minutes longer. They discussed how Eden was feeling in her body more than her head. About how December always seems to speed up right when you want it to slow down. They also discussed Donovan's daughter.

Satisfied with the updates from the night before, Amara shifted, adding another layer to their conversation.

"Katy called me. She told me about her plan."

Eden exhaled and closed her eyes, "Figures."

"She couldn't reach you, so she called me. She was worried you'd feel manipulated."

"I did," Eden said plainly.

Amara hummed. "Sometimes people don't conspire against us. They conspire *for* us because they see something we're still learning how to hold. Have you ever thought about that?"

Eden leaned back in her chair as Amara's words wash over her.

"Yeah but." Eden said.

"Yeah, but what Eden," Amara interjected. "You need to figure out what part you're really upset about. And then let this go."

Eden slowed down her words, "I mean. This all now feels fake. I knew it was too good to be true and now it doesn't feel real."

Amara spoke through her clenched teeth trying to maintain restraint. "Eden, please get your life. This is a good thing. Let it be a good thing. And I'm done with that."

"Also," Amara continued, lighter now, "I'm going to keep asking until I get an answer because time is flying by. What are we doing for your birthday?"

The familiar instinct to deflect rose quickly. But something else answered first.

"I still don't know yet," she said slowly. "BUT I've been thinking. Not like a party but something that feels like me. I just don't know what that is yet."

Amara smiled through the phone. Eden could hear it. "Well, that's new. I'll take it."

"I know right." Eden replied.

Just as their call was ending, an email notification appeared.

A request for the day off...from Katy.

Eden didn't fill the silence with stories or assumptions. She let it be what it was. Some things needed time to reenter on their own. She approved the request and checked her phone to find a text from Donovan.

Donovan: I'm headed over to your office.

Within minutes, Donovan and Marcel arrived together, coats in hand, moving with the ease of men who understood timing.

At her half-open door, Donovan smiled as soon as he saw Eden. "Can we come in?"

Eden looked up and smiled back at the first sight of Donovan, "Sure, come on in."

Marcel entered quietly, eyes lowered at first, careful of his presence. Eden met his gaze briefly and softened her expression just enough. He nodded once. It was enough.

Based on how he and Katy conspired with their plan and updated each other regularly, she knew, he'd report back to Katy as fast as humanly possible.

No one mentioned the weekend or anything that might feel like a fault line.

"It's Day Thirteen," Donovan said, handing her an envelope. "Here's your gift beautiful lady. For later today, when your body wants something kind."

Inside the envelope was a gift card to a smoothie shop nearby.

"This is for restoring," he added.

Eden's eyes met his. He wasn't watching for her reaction. He was offering, then letting go.

"Thank you," she said, meaning more than just the card.

"My pleasure," he replied, holding her look a beat longer than necessary. "I'll call you later."

After they left, Eden didn't rush back into doing work. She stood, stretched her arms overhead and felt her spine respond.

Restore your body, the day seemed to whisper. Not as a command. An invitation.

She sat down and searched her inbox and found the email she'd been ignoring. Her Pilates membership renewal. She accepted the retention offer right then.

Walking out for a break, she walked down to the smoothie shop. She ordered something green and grounding and drank it slowly.

It'd been a while since she'd chosen her body, not as something to override, but something to cherish.

On Day Thirteen, with Jubilee approaching, she chose restoration for her body.

Chapter 24

The office no longer felt like a place of momentum. Instead, it felt like a place of endings.

Desks stood half-cleared, coffee mugs rinsed and left upside down as if saying goodbye.

Eden moved through the building with a sense of urgency that wasn't flanked by panic, but stewardship. Her heels clicked faster than usual. Her bag felt heavier than it needed to be. She was a woman on a mission. She wanted to leave nothing unfinished.

This was the last full week before the holidays thinned the halls completely, and without Katy, the silence was louder.

The gaps showed up in small ways. The absence of Katy's chair rolling towards her doorway with a question already half-answered. The way her calendar felt heavier without a second set of eyes guarding it.

An email notification popped up.

Another time-off request.

From Katy.

Eden read it once. Then once again. She approved it without cere-mony or any commentary.

Not everything requires a reaction.

Rolling her shoulders back, inhaling deeply, she closed her eyes for a moment. Her body had begun asking to be acknowledged lately, and she was listening.

"Even though Katy's not coming in today, I can still get some things done before I have to leave for this luncheon." She said.

The luncheon reminder popped up on her screen. The few hours she worked felt like minutes. It was time to go.

Gathering her things for the foundation's board nomination lun-cheon, she said to herself, "Okay. Let's go see what this is all about."

Inside the restaurant, it was dressed for December without being festive about it. It was elegant in the way money pretended not to notice itself. White tablecloths. Soft lighting. Conversations pitched just low enough to feel important.

Eden adjusted her coat as she entered, scanning the room with practiced ease.

Donovan was already there.

He looked up as though he felt her before he saw her.

Walking towards him, he pulled out the chair beside him, as though her seating had already been decided.

"You look like you're carrying the entire year in that bag," he said reaching to alleviate the bag from her shoulder. "Here, let me help you with that."

Their shoulders brushed as he assisted and they settled. The contact was brief but around them, people noticed. Not in a gossiping way, in a way that quietly recalibrated assumptions.

The luncheon was for the potential new class of nominated board members. There were faces from all over, a full and diverse crowd from various organizations across the city.

The luncheon unfolded with practiced rhythm, board expectations and the selection process, speeches filled with gratitude, and vision cast for the future.

Eden spoke when invited, her voice carrying both authority and ease. Donovan watched her the way people do when they're quietly proud. Visibility suited her. She was in her element.

When he spoke, she did the same.

When the networking began, a man Eden hadn't met made a bee-line for Donovan.

Extending his hand to Donovan, he said, "I'm Nathanial. It's nice to meet you. I've heard great things about your work. You know," he said lowering his voice with false intimacy, "with board seats opening up, due diligence becomes...essential."

Donovan turned to him fully.

"I've heard things," the man continued, smiling thinly. "About Eden's past. There was an incident a few years ago. It's resurfacing now that her name is circulating."

Donovan didn't interrupt.

"It's not criminal or anything like that, oh no," the man quickly added. "But perception matters. You know what I mean? Especially for donors. I would hate for my nomination and appointment to be associated with something like this. Some of us just want to be cautious."

Cautious was the word people used when they wanted to wound without consequences.

A few of us are getting together later for drinks to discuss the optics of her being on the board. Nothing crazy, we just want to hash out our concerns."

Concern. The most respectable form of sabotage.

What he wasn't telling Donovan was that, he was the only one with concerns. This wasn't a big secret being shared. This was a narrative being deployed. Strategically and to anyone who would listen.

Except Eden.

Across the room, she was mid-sentence, explaining a program expansion with the founder's wife, completely unaware of the undercurrent attempting to rewrite her.

"Thank you for the information," he said evenly. "I'll take this under advisement."

The man nodded, satisfied, and leaned back, scanning the room for his next audience.

As the luncheon ended, Eden and Donovan walked out together in the sharp and honest December air.

"What a luncheon huh? I guess we'll find out if we are appointed next week." Eden said.

"Yes," he said, his voice flatter than before. "Very informative."

"Are you okay?" Eden said, glancing at Donovan as they reached the sidewalk.

"Yes, I'm fine," he smiled. "Just thinking."

Eden nodded. She didn't pry. Trust had begun to live between them without explanation.

Before parting ways, he said, "I know you're trying to get back to work but here." He said handing her a small gift bag.

"Ahh, what is it?"

"Uh, let's just say, it's a place to remember where you came from and tell *your* story in a different way."

She studied him. "That sounds ominous."

"It's not," he said softly. "You'll see when you open it. I hope you like it and get where I was coming from when I chose it."

Eden reached in and hugged Donovan. His hugs were generally stronger than this one. Still he looked down at her and smiled saying, "Enjoy the rest of your day and I'll call you later."

Back at her office, Eden worked with intention. She closed projects. She sent final emails. She let go of what could wait.

Releasing a sigh of completion, Eden opened the gift from Donovan.

The notecard for today's gift was handwritten by Donovan.

Day 14: Return to your story. Go back to the origin and imagine God narrating it, telling your truth with tenderness.

The gift was a small journal she could write freely. She allowed herself to feel the story first before she wrote in it.

Somewhere across the city, Donovan found himself in rooms with other potential board members quietly rallying against Eden.

He fielded conversation he hadn't asked for, listening as people attempted to define Eden without knowing her. He said little but learned a lot. He read the room instantly; he knew a witch hunt when he saw one.

He had always known visibility came with a price.

The question now at hand was never about whether Eden could withstand it.

It was about who would stand beside her when it arrived.

Chapter 25

Waking before the chimes of her alarm, Eden stretched, listening to her breath, noticing how her body felt rested instead of blocked.

On impulse, she reached for her phone, charging next to Laurence's letter on the nightstand.

Breakfast before work? She typed the message to Donovan. She hesitated just long enough to wonder why she was asking, then sent it anyway.

The dots indicating he was responding back popped up on her phone almost immediately.

Today must be my lucky day. I was hoping you'd ask.

With a plan in place to meet at a small breakfast diner in between both of their offices, they both hopped up to get ready.

The diner was the kind of place that smelled like coffee was poured with care. There was no music competing for attention. Just clinking of mugs and clanks of kitchen utensils flipping on the grill.

Donovan stood when he saw her, smiling like this was exactly where he wanted to be, planting a kiss on her cheek as they embraced for a good morning hug.

"Well, this was spontaneous, huh?" She said as she sat.

"I like spontaneous. I'm huge quotes guy and Germaine Greer once said, 'The essence of pleasure is spontaneity,' and it is my pleasure to be here with you."

Eden smiled. Somehow, the quote legitimized her nudging. It marked a rare thing for her: initiating connection. Her body and spirit were in agreement. She wanted him near.

They ordered simple. Eggs, toast, coffee...food meant to steady the day, not bury it.

With everything they'd experienced over the last several days, conversation was easy, full, and vibrant.

"Yeah man, I told you last night when we were talking, the office is so quiet, I heard something fall and I jumped up so fast, like who did that? Because I'm practically the only one there. Well, Marcel is still there, because I am."

Eden tried to compose herself. She'd just taken a huge bite of fluffy eggs but imaging Donovan jumping up in alarm was too funny. Then, in the next instance, she nodded her head acknowledging he had his assistant, but she didn't have hers.

Donovan looked at Eden and then reached over into his coat pocket that was lying across the booth. He placed a small, beautifully wrapped gift box on the table between them.

"This is for today," he said gently. "Open the note later. But the gift is...this."

Opening the box, Eden found a handkerchief.

It wasn't new but it was delicate, softened with use, now clean and pressed with meaning.

Eden looked at it, then at him.

Picking up the handkerchief, running her fingers along the fabric and lace, she asked, "What's today's theme?"

"Closing the door," he said. "On betrayal."

He didn't flinch when he said the word and neither did she when she heard it.

"Not the events of betrayal," he continued. "The energy of it. The agreements you didn't know you made when you were young. The ones that said you had to overperform in order to survive."

Eden's throat tightened but she didn't look away.

"Today is about the woman who handles betrayal well in public," he said softly. "But collapses in private."

There it was.

This wasn't an accusation, it was recognition.

"Are you trying to make me have to use this gift now?" She asked with her eyes on the brink of tears.

"No, that's not my intent but if you need to, go ahead." He said with comfort.

"I never and I mean never let anyone see that part of me," she declared.

"I know," he replied. "But this isn't about exposing you, it's about releasing you."

As his coffee refill arrived, the steam rising between them grounded the moment.

After a moment, she said, "So you invited me to your parents' house. Now I would like to invite you to mine.

Donovan perked up and it wasn't from the jolt of caffeine.

"It is nothing big, but my parents want to have a birthday memorial for what would have been my godfather's 100th birthday. It matters to me."

With a reverential nod, he said, "If it matters to you, it matters to me. I'd be honored."

Work was starting to signal this was still a workday as both of their phones were constantly buzzing.

"I guess we need to get to it, but I have enjoyed this and spending the first part of my morning with you." Eden said.

As they walked out, Donovan said, "This has been a perfect start to my day." He said opening the door. "Go and get your work done. Do work you'd be proud of today, Eden. I'll check in with you later."

Outside of the diner, Eden noticed how the door swung shut behind them. It didn't slam. It didn't linger. It simply closed, sealing the warmth inside.

"Okay," she said. "Have a good day."

They shared a hug, he walked to his office, and she walked to hers.

With each passing day, the office staff was shrinking. Katy's desk was still empty. Back at the diner, Eden approved another time-off request.

At lunch, she walked into a quiet conference room, she unfolded the handkerchief again and read the note Donovan had tucked away, written in his handwriting.

Day 15: Closing the Door. It wasn't your fault. For the first and last time, name the betrayals without rehearsing them. Notice the patterns that formed as you learned to survive. Acknowledge them and then release them. When the memories rise, don't hide. Wipe your tears and say goodbye to those emotions and the energy. Stand up and leave the room, closing the door behind you.

A handkerchief was the perfect gift for that assignment. It is a visual representation that you are allowed to be seen with your grief and it gives permission for tears.

And she would need it as her soft and honest tears fell.

She didn't feel the need to crawl under the covers, or disappear, or pour a drink.

She sat in the power of her own emotions.

The tears continued to come. And she let them.

Standing to walk back to her office. She closed the conference room door, leaving that part of herself behind and felt her shoulders settle.

She was not just closing the door on betrayal and its impact on her life. She was closing a door on an identity fragment.

Outside of the door, she sent Donovan a text.

Donovan: Thank you for today.

Chapter 26

Eden paused, breathing in the faint scent of the candle she'd just lit, labeled Vintage Christmas. It was a tiny ritual for clarity before the day began.

She hadn't touched her emails, yet when Marcel appeared at the door, his quiet shadow framed there. He stood holding a package and a card, wrapped with care.

"Hi. Can I come in?" he said knocking lightly.

Eden looked up surprised. "Oh hi! Sure. Come on in."

"Delivery for you," Marcel said, setting the package down gently on her desk.

"For me?" she said, even as she tried to sound surprised. By now, the gifts had trained her to expect the unexpected.

He nodded, a small, knowing smile tugged at his lips. "Donovan asked me to make sure you got this before you got too busy with your day. He said today's theme is Renew Your Relationships."

Excited to see what the day's gift might be, she curiously opened the package.

Inside was a delicate picture frame. The image was a placeholder, and a gift card taped to the back. The frame was simple, yet elegant, white with subtle gold trim. The frame invited presence without demanding perfection.

Her eyes lifted to Marcel. "A lunch...for someone I choose huh?"

"Exactly. You are to choose someone who pours into you. That is all the instruction he gave," he said. "He trusts you'll know how to proceed."

Eden's chest warmed with the quiet care embedded in the gift. She turned the frame in her hands, fingers tracing the gold trim, thinking about its emptiness and who she would fill the frame with.

A notification on his smart watch alerted to a very important appearance.

Offering a slow nod, he said, "Well, I'll leave you to it. I just got a text Katy's walking in the building. I'd like to go down and meet her. Have a good day, Eden."

She nodded, taking in a deep breath, "Thank you Marcel and the same to you."

The office building shifted the moment Katy entered. Those there for work, heralded her return, "Hi Katy!"

Katy walked past Eden's office, hands tucked tightly around her bag strap, with her posture slightly guarded.

She couldn't pass without being noticed.

"Katy," Eden said softly, standing.

Katy paused and turned around standing a hair outside of Eden's office watching her standing behind her desk.

They stood watching each other without saying anything. The air between them was careful, not heavy. The silence didn't press; it recalibrated them.

"Good morning," they both said.

Katy walked in and broke the initial barrier, "Eden. I...I wanted to," she stopped herself, glancing at Eden's desk between them. She was searching for permission, learning to ask before assuming.

Gesturing towards the chair in front of her. "Sit. Let's...just start there."

"I know a lot happened while I was gone. I didn't...I didn't want to overstep."

Eden shook her head, smiling lightly, "You're here now. That's what matters."

Katy exhaled, relief softening her features. "Thank you, Eden. Really."

Eden's fingers brushed the gifted frame sitting on her desk. She lifted it somewhat. "I have something for you," she said. "Well, technically, it was meant for me. But I think today, it belongs to both of us."

Katy shifted her head to the right.

"It's a reminder," Eden continued, "to renew what matters. To spend time with someone who pours into you. And maybe, just maybe try and capture it, in some way."

She raised the gift card towards Katy. "We're going to do lunch together, soon."

"I just want to say this," Katy began. "I saw an opportunity and jumped on it. I thought I was doing something special. I didn't ask because I was afraid, you'd say no."

Katy's words offered a confession, and Eden didn't rescue her from it.

Eden's eyes glistened, and a small laugh escaped her. "If we're both being honest; I didn't know how to trust good things could arrive without help."

Katy's heart lightened.

They talked through the morning, laughter punctuating their conversation. Stories were shared and acknowledgements were made without fanfare. An exchange was taking place between two women who'd weathered some storms and were now leaning into each other again.

Katy wasn't just an assistant. She had been a co-regulator, a gate-keeper, a proxy voice. When that trust fractured, Eden didn't just lose help. She lost ground.

Eden reached across the desk to hold Katy's hand for a brief moment. "I want you at my parents' house this evening," she said. "For Laurence's birthday memorial. I'd love it if you could come?"

Katy's expression shifted to tenderness and respect. "I'll be there," she said. "And...Marcel?"

"Yes, of course." Eden replied.

The breach had been repaired, and their entire ecosystem had been restored.

"I'm going to get my day started. I'm glad we were able to talk. Can I bring anything tonight for the memorial?" Katy said.

"No need to bring anything but your beautiful selves and I'm glad we were able to talk as well."

Katy picked up her things and walked out.

Eden looks at the frame once more. She decided to let it sit empty for a while. She knows she and Katy will fill it with the right picture because renewal isn't rushed.

And because she was learning good things can arrive even when she didn't push them through herself.

Chapter 27

The house smelled like orange peels, cloves, and something slow roasting in the oven. Eden stood at the kitchen counter with her mother, Liora, watching her hands move with ease. There was no recipe open, no measuring cups in sight. Just memory guiding the motions.

"Laurence always liked things simple," Liora said, slicing a loaf of freshly made bread. "Good bread, real butter, and a table where people could sit as long as they wanted."

Eden nodded, smoothing the tablecloth she had ironed earlier that afternoon. She stood quietly, thinking of Laurence and his birthday. She thanked him for the letter, for seeing her, and for always encouraging her to always persevere. A few tears slipped down her cheeks.

Outside, dusk settled early. December had a way of pulling the light close, like it wanted to be held.

The first knock at the door came just after six.

Amara and Grant arrived bundled in scarves and laughter, arms full of containers and an unapologetic bag of Christmas candy.

Donovan arrived next, standing a half step back from the door when Eden opened it, as if giving her space, even now.

He pulled her into a hug with one arm and held a single white candle in a gift bag with the other.

"For Laurence," he whispered.

"Thank you."

Katy and Marcel came together and walked up right behind Donovan. Marcel carried a bottle of wine. Katy held a small plate of cookies she admitted to almost burned but saved just in time.

"I wasn't sure what to bring," Katy said.

"Which is exactly why I told you to just bring yourselves. You're here, and that's perfect." Eden replied.

Marcel smiled at that. There was something unspoken passing among their quartet, a recognition of restoration.

Then Eden heard her father's voice.

"Come in out of the cold," John said with the kind of voice that didn't rush a room but grounded it. "Laurence hated drafts."

Everyone laughed as coats were hung, dishes placed, and drinks poured.

Eden took Donovan straight away to meet her parents.

"Mama, daddy, I'd like for you to meet Donovan." Eden said.

Donovan extended his hand but both John and Liora stood extending arms for hugs.

"Oh nonsense, we're huggers around here." They said.

Eden stood by watching her parents embrace and welcome Donovan into their home.

In the living room, a table had been set up. On it sat a framed photo of Laurence in his younger years. Another framed photo showed Laurence standing with Millie, John and Liora, with one hand resting on Eden's shoulder. She couldn't have been more than five.

Donovan stood there for a moment, taking in the photos. Eden noticed.

"He taught me how to ride a bike," she said, joining Donovan. "He let go before I knew he had."

"That's the best kind of teacher."

When everyone settled, John cleared his throat. He didn't stand and he didn't raise his glass yet. He waited until the room quieted on its own.

"Laurence used to say," John began, "that a good life doesn't announce itself. It shows up. Every day. Especially when it could be easier not to."

Those words landed differently for everyone.

"He was Eden's godfather on paper. But in practice, he was a steady presence. He and Millie paid attention. They remembered birthdays and small details that mattered more than big gestures ever could."

John glanced at his daughter.

"Laurence believed in showing love early. We miss our dear old friend and wanted to simply honor him today on what would have been his one hundredth birthday."

Liora reached for her husband's hand.

"To Laurence," John said, raising his glass.

"To Laurence," the room echoed.

The candle Donovan brough was lit and placed beside the photos.

Conversations resumed gently. More stories of the good old days surfaced like Christmas gifts. Laurence's stubborn loyalty and his dry humor came up more than once.

Amara made her way around the room, inviting everyone to their Christmas Eve party.

"We're hosting Christmas Eve this year. Think s'mores, Christmas Karaoke, ridiculous games, ugly sweaters, white elephant gift exchange, all the food and drink you can think of. No pressure. But we'd love you there."

"My wife is in a festive frenzy. I'm hoping to survive the next few days." Grant said laughing.

Katy laughed with her shoulders relaxing. Marcel nudged her slightly as he felt part of the rhythm of the room.

Later, as the guests started to thin, Eden found Donovan in the kitchen with Liora, helping to clean.

Eden paused in the archway folding her arms across her chest to observe a beautiful sight. Donovan rinsed plates beside Liora, sleeves rolled up, listening more than he spoke.

"Mama, do you mind if I borrow Donovan for a minute?"

"No, go right ahead. I'm almost finished in here."

Eden grabbed his hand and stepped outside on the porch. The air was sharp; their breath was visible. They surveyed the neighborhood, smiling as Christmas lights glowed from nearby houses.

"You okay?" he asked.

"I'm better than okay."

They stood side by side, not touching, just sharing the moment.

"Thank you for coming tonight. You know, I didn't realize how much Laurence shaped my idea of love. He was dependable and kind and I had forgotten that."

Turning toward her, Donovan said, "That kind of love leaves a mark."

"Yes, it does." Eden said looking up at Donovan. Without asking permission from old fears, Eden reached for him.

The kiss was gentle, a meeting rather than a taking.

When they pulled back, she rested her head against his chest, listening for his heartbeat.

He stood holding her, steady without crowding but covering. She let herself rest there, receiving the sound his heartbeat was making for her.

Chapter 28

K aty walked briskly toward the office building, her bag strap
sliding comfortably over her shoulder. The icy December air
brushed against her cheeks with a faint bite of frost. Her breath rose
in little clouds as she approached the building.

"Katy," a familiar voice called.

Christopher hurried to catch up, slightly winded. "Raccoon Katy!"

Stepping into the warmth of the building, Katy turned to see
Christopher.

"Christopher?" she said cautiously, slowing down.

"Yes, it's me and I know," he said quickly raising his hands. "I know
I'm...unexpected. But I was hoping I could talk to you?"

"About what?"

"I want to do something special for Eden," he said, pausing as if he
was expecting a reaction. "Her birthday. Christmas. Or both. I was
hoping you could help me plan it."

Katy's eyes narrowed, not in judgement but in maturity. "That's a
hard no for me," she said firmly.

"But why?" he asked, frowning. "I've freed of my schedule for the rest of the year and I really would like to surprise her and get something nice."

"I don't need to explain that," she replied. "And she doesn't need someone trying to control how good things arrive."

Christopher opened his mouth, but she cut him off. "Look, I'm not the person to help you with this. Sorry. But not for real."

Christopher's shoulders sank. "Right," he said, with a much-lowered voice. "I see."

"Happy holidays, Christopher. Goodbye." Katy said giving him a polite but strong smile. She stood and watched him turn and leave the building.

Inside, it was the last official day before Christmas break, and the building seemed to exhale a collective agreement.

Eden arrived early, not out of obligation but she had plans with Donovan for dinner, so she wanted to wrap up her day efficiently.

After the holiday luncheon, she planned to send her final emails, set her out-of-office reply, and say goodbye to the office for the year.

She was genuinely happy, looking forward to the holiday season in a way she hadn't expected.

Donovan had been doing all of the gift giving but she started thinking about what she would give him for Christmas.

Browsing online for gifts, she found herself overwhelmed by the thought of finding something meaningful for him.

***

Donovan stood when she arrived, grinning like he'd been waiting all day for this exact moment.

"You look incredible," he said as they sat.

"I feel incredible," she said. "It's Christmas break baby, whoo hoo. How'd the rest of your day go today?"

"After you agreed to dinner, it went smooth sailing." He said teasing. "How about you?"

"It went well. We are well positioned with the revitalization project in the new year. I know I could not have completed this project without you and I am so grateful." She said.

Taking her hand in his to kiss it, he said, "It has been my absolute pleasure collaborating with you. Best Christmas present ever."

Eden dropped her head back, him saying that wasn't going to help her with what to get him for an actual Christmas gift.

They ordered slowly and talked easily. Without the scaffolding of work around them, their conversations softened. Laughter lingered and soft touches and longer glances became the norm.

At one point, Donovan leaned back, watching her with that thoughtful look she was beginning to recognize.

"Are you ready for today's gift?" he asked.

"Can I ask you something first?"

"Sure?"

"How long is this going to last? Are you planning to give me gifts for the rest of my life?" she asked.

"Now that depends on you," he said coyly. "However, this gifting plan goes until your birthday. And you still have not told me what you want to do yet?"

"Why are you asking, do you want to plan it?" She said in somewhat of a flirtatious, playful way.

"I most certainly can, if that's what you want."

"I have started thinking about how I'd like to celebrate. I haven't finalized anything, but I know I want you there. No matter what the plan is."

"That's fair and I'm more than good with that." He said. "Can I give you your gift for today now?"

"Yes, please," she said, already curious.

"Well first, the theme is Renew Your Confidence. You are to say out loud what you already know is true."

She didn't ask for clarification.

Instead, she tilted her head, allowing a playful sparkle to enter her eyes.

"You want me to say it...now?" she asked.

"I do," he smiled.

Eden took a natural, deep breath.

With her head and shoulders pulled back and chest front and center, she declared, "I know I am deeply loved. I know I don't chase what is meant for me. And I know...I am not too much."

She stopped, then added one more.

"I know I'm exactly enough."

Donovan did not say anything at first. He just looked at her, his eyes warm and proud.

"Yeah, that sounds about right."

As they lingered over dessert, he pulled out a small envelope from his coat pocket.

"Here's today's gift," he said, sliding it across the table. "Well. The promise of it."

The card inside read:

A photoshoot tomorrow with something very special to me.

Eden looked up. "A photographer?"

"Yes. It's actually my daughter," he said watching her carefully. "She is kind of a big deal photographer. The night you met her at Merrykah was her first night home on winter break. She's been staying with her mother. I did not want to overwhelm you with all of this, so I waited. But she agreed to do the shoot. It was her idea."

Eden felt honored.

"Wow, that's incredibly thoughtful. From you both."

He kissed her hand once more. "You're not wrong."

"Tomorrow, you said. I'd love to."

Covering her hand with his, he said, "I want you to have a record of this version of yourself. The one who is confident enough to know."

Eden rested in the realization confidence is lived without apology when one trusts what they know to be true.

And Donovan... was the truth.

Chapter 29

"Good morning, Mama," Eden answered, half asleep, half awake, yet somehow already energized.

On the other end, Liora was wide awake and fully in motion. She was calling to recap Laurence's birthday memorial.

"Everything went well the other night for Laurence. What do you think? It looked like everyone had a wonderful time." Liora said.

"I think so," Eden replied, stifling a yawn.

Noticing Eden's slower tempo, Liora softened, "Did I wake you?"

"Not really. I was just being a little lazy, but I was about to get up anyway. I have a photoshoot this morning, courtesy of Donovan." Eden said, slipping into the tone she reserved for best-friend conversations.

"My, my, my. That Donovan is something else. Your father and I really enjoyed him." Liora said. "So, you say he's doing a photoshoot for you?"

"He arranged it. His daughter's the photographer. I'm just supposed to show up. There's a whole glam squad and a stylist bringing options for me. I'm really excited. It sounds like it's going to be a lot of fun."

"That sounds lovely." Liora said, then paused, her tone shifting. "Well, I was also calling because I wanted to tell you something."

"Oh yeah? Eden said lightly. "Tell me something good. I don't want to hear nothing bad."

"I think it *is* good." Liora said, chuckling. "That old heifer called me again."

Eden sat straight up in her bed.

"Marie? Boris' mother?"

"The one and only."

"Did you answer? What did she want?"

"I don't know. When my phone rang and I saw the caller ID, I frowned so hard my face hurt. And here's the part I wanted to tell you," Liora said, her voice lifting. I deleted *and* blocked her number. All by myself."

"Oh, look at you," Eden teased. "Learning how to use your new cellphone."

"Yes! I was very proud of myself for figuring it out. But more than that, some calls don't need to be answered. And hers won't be anymore."

"I'm proud of you too, Mama."

"And I'm proud of you baby," Liora said, her voice warm with joy. "You're shining so bright and I love that for you."

In true Liora fashion, she wrapped things up before Eden could. "Now go on and get up for your little photoshoot. Send me pictures so I can see them on my new phone."

Eden was quite tickled and replied, "Will do, Mama. Bye."

The photoshoot was set inside a massive warehouse. From the outside, it gave nothing away. Inside, it was pure magic.

Krista was already there, coffee in hand, radiating warmth and effortless confidence as she spoke with the glam team she'd curated for Eden.

Stepping into Krista's world felt Eden stepping natural, safe, and playful.

"Eden. Hi, good morning." Krista said smiling. "Come on in. You can put your things over there. They are ready for you."

Krista moved with ease, directing the flow, checking details, making sure everything was right.

As Eden settled into the makeup chair, Krista reappeared holding a vase overflowing with red roses.

"Dad just had these delivered," she said, placing them gently on the beauty table in front of Eden.

"Oh my God," Eden laughed. "I'm so glad you haven't put my lashes on yet, because I would've cried them right off."

The glam squad worked their magic. By the time they stepped back, Eden barely recognized herself.

"Okay," Krista said, adjusting her camera strap. "We'll start off easy. I am going to do a few test shots to check the lighting."

She guided Eden into position.

"Alright, Eden. Forget the camera is here. Pretend you are moving through a regular day. Breathe and have fun."

And Eden did just that.

She laughed more than she could remember. Between shots, she and Krista talked. The mood shifting until it felt less like a photoshoot and more like time spent with an old friend.

Krista lowered her camera suddenly. "Whatever you just did with your shoulders? Do that again."

Eden laughed, shrugging. "I don't even know what I did."

"Precisely." Krista said, snapping the shot. "That's the magic."

They continued, conversation flowing.

"So," Krista said casually, "my boyfriend's coming into town tonight."

Eden's face lit up. Krista captured it instantly.

"That's exciting."

'Exciting and mildly terrifying." Krista admitted. "I'm introducing him to my family. Did you hear that? *My family*. The one you met the other night."

Eden winced in solidarity. "Oh. Yeah. Okay. But it could still be fun."

Krista laughed. "You've met my dad, right?"

"I have," Eden said, smiling. "And honestly? He's wonderful. Most people end up choosing partners like their parents. If Donovan's the blueprint, I wouldn't expect you to have any trouble."

Krista kept snapping.

"He's wonderful *now*," she said gently. "But he wasn't always. He was and still is an excellent provider. That was never the issue," Krista continued with her truth. "When I was younger, work came first. And *other* things. Back then, love was more transactional."

Eden absorbed Krista's words quietly.

"He used to apologize all the time. But it got to a point where I told him to stop because he had worn out sorry a long time ago."

Eden felt those words chip at her heart.

"But he's changed," Krista added. "Especially in the last year and a half. He shows up differently now. I think it has been healing for both of us. He is just still...very intense about who I bring around."

Eden could feel the truth in what Krista was saying.

Well," Eden said, warmth rising instinctively, "then why don't you all come to my place tonight? Dinner. Low pressure."

The words escaped before her brain could catch them.

Krista's face lit up. "Really?"

"Yes," Eden said, confidence sprinting ahead of logistics. "Absolutely."

They stared at each other for half a second.

Then Eden's eyes widened.

Oh no.

Her house was undecorated. No tree. No wreath. No twinkling lights. She had not hosted anyone since Boris. She did not cook. She barely owned *groceries*.

Krista hugged her, blissfully unaware of the internal spiral happening. "Thank you. That means so much."

Eden smiled and held it while maintaining eye contact.

"I think we have some amazing shots." Krista said, setting her camera down." And since you just agreed to host dinner tonight, I think we are done here."

The moment Krista turned away, Eden grabbed her phone.

Katy answered on the first ring.

"Hold on." Eden said, dialing Amara.

With everyone on the line, Eden whispered in a high-pitched frequency, "9-1-1 emergency."

"I love emergencies," Katy said immediately.

"Krista. Donovan. Boyfriend. Dinner. Tonight. My house. I don't cook. Help!"

Silence.

Katy said, "Don't worry. I'm on my way."

"Say less," Amara followed, after Eden's rushed explanation. "I'll bring wine. And decorations. And of course, the vibes."

Within the hour, the three of them were reunited in Eden's kitchen like a tactical unit.

Sizing up the space, Katy said, "Okay. This isn't bad. We have worked with worse."

"Have we?" Eden asked.

"Yes...remember Thanksgiving last year?" Katy said.

Amara laughed, pulling garland from a rolling cart. "We are not repeating history here tonight, we're making it."

They moved fast. Katy delegated like a Christmas general. Amara danced through the rooms, singing while hanging lights.

Eden ran to the store twice, buying things she didn't need and forgetting half the things she did.

Katy held up a decorative pillow out of one of the bags. Why does this say *Blessed & Busy*?"

"I don't know. I panicked. I was just grabbing stuff." Eden said laughing.

"I understand," Katy smirked.

Laughter filled Eden's home, the kind that resets nervous systems and reminds women who they are to each other.

"This," Amara said, holding a glass up, "is why we don't do life alone."

Eden looked around at them with a full heart. Her home was magazine worthy and ready to receive guests again.

"Thank you for being here and helping me." She said. "Are y'all going to come by for the dinner?"

"Katy grinned. "Please. This is what we do. I can't. Marcel and I have plans."

"Like your pillow says, I'm booked and blessed. We'll have to catch you on the flip." Amara said.

The trio hugged, and then Eden was alone again. But this time, she wouldn't be alone for long.

Chapter 30

Eden's house never sounded like this.

Poinsettias lined the entryway, and the mingled scent of pine and vanilla wrapped itself around everyone who stepped inside.

Laughter bounced off the walls. Christmas music played low in the background. There was the clink of glasses, the scrape of chairs, the unmistakable comfort of people settling in and deciding to stay a while.

It felt lived in.

Donovan stood near the kitchen island, sleeves rolled up, watching Eden move between Krista and Daniel. There was a lightness to her that made him smile.

Eden still wore the glow from the photoshoot earlier that day. Her makeup was flawless, but the rest of her shifted into something more relaxed. A Feliz Navidad T-shirt, jeans, and a Santa hat perched slightly on her head.

"Oh, Santa baby." Donovan said, pulling her into a hug and pressing a kiss to her cheek.

Eden laughed, warmed, and unguarded.

"So far, this is officially my favorite Eden." Krista said, snapping a candid photo with her phone.

"Oh no. You're taking pictures? Are you working?" Eden asked.

"These are strictly personal," Krista replied. "You're safe. For now."

"Let's eat while the food is still hot," Eden said, steering everyone toward the dining room table.

Dinner unfolded easily. Conversations overlapped, while inside jokes began forming in real time. There was no awkwardness, no polite distance.

Halfway through the meal, Eden leaned back in her chair, "I do have dessert," she said, then paused. "But I came up with a better idea. How do we feel about a cookie baking and decorating contest?"

Krista clapped once, delighted. "A little Christmas competition between couples? I'm already obsessed."

Daniel leaned in. "We're absolutely winning."

"Bold words, son," Donovan said, amused. "Very bold."

The kitchen transformed.

Flour dusted the counters. Frosting lids popped open. Sprinkles spilled everywhere and no one cared. Laughter filled the space as they took the competition far more seriously than necessary.

Eden felt Donovan's presence constantly, behind her, beside her, occasionally brushing past her as they reached for the same towel or tray. She leaned in to whisper something dry and funny in his ear. Her breath warmed his skin.

Krista could not help herself. She grabbed her camera again, capturing the chemistry unfolding naturally between them.

The cookies themselves were...expressive. Stars, trees, and a snowman Eden insisted had character despite its uneven smile.

As they worked, Donovan's eyes drifted to the trash can. It was full. Overflowing, actually. Bags from earlier sat beside it, evidence of a woman who had poured herself into making an ordinary Saturday night feel intentional.

He didn't say a word.

He tied the bags, lifted them easily, and took them outside as if it were the most natural thing in the world.

Inside, Krista was laughing, mid-story. "My dad has this whole collection of vintage comic books," she said to Daniel. "First editions, like rare finds. It is totally his thing."

When Donovan returned, Eden was laughing so hard at Krista she had to steady herself on the counter.

Once the cookies were judged a tie, Eden disappeared briefly and returned with small linen bags tied with ribbons.

"Dinner party favors," Eden said, handing them out.

Krista opened hers first. "Stop it. These are so adorable. Thank you, Eden."

Donovan watched Eden as she moved around the room, thoughtful in ways she never announced.

Krista's excitement reached a new level. "Girl, I couldn't wait," she said, already unlocking her phone. "Your photos are fire! I edited them earlier."

Krista mirrored her screen to Eden's television, and the room went quiet for a moment as the images appeared.

"Wow," Daniel said. "Those are stunning. You really captured her babe."

Krista grinned. "Well, she made it easy."

More photos followed. Candids of everyone together. Then a few of Eden and Donovan near the Christmas tree Katy and Amare conjured earlier that evening.

"So," Krista said causally, "Grandma has voluntold all of us we are going to church tomorrow. Eden, are you coming with us?"

"This is the first time I'm hearing of it."

Donovan met her eyes. "You know now. Wanna go?" Donovan asked.

They all looked at her, waiting.

"I guess I'm going to church tomorrow." Eden said.

Later, belongings were gathered, hugs exchanged, and promises made.

Krista hugged Eden tightly. "Thank you for tonight. Seriously." She leaned in and whispered, "He's lighter around you. You bring that out in him."

Daniel followed with a smile, "This was really something. It was nice meeting you both. I had a great time."

Donovan lingered after the door closed behind them.

"You were amazing tonight," he said.

"So were you."

Donovan jumped up quickly, ""Before I forget. It is late, but I want to give you today's gift. The theme is finances."

Inside the wrapped gift, Eden found the latest financial wellness book everyone has been talking about. She ran her fingers over the cover, feeling the thought behind it.

Watching her closely, "I'm not trying to manage anything for you," he said gently. "This is just support. The assignment is to write down something you're worried about financially. Then write what you're believing instead."

"I love this." She said, kissing his cheek.

After Donovan left, the house grew quiet again. Eden moved through it slowly, collecting stray glasses, smiling at the echoes of the evening.

Her phone buzzed.

She glanced down.

Krista tagged her in a post from her professional accounts. Eden's photos filled the screen. Her notifications exploded. Likes. Comments. Shares. Old names resurfacing. New eyes watching. A familiar tightness brushed through Eden's chest.

Then another message came through.

Christopher: *Can we please meet Monday morning? Our spot.*

Eden stared at the screen for a long time.

Then she set her phone to Do Not Disturb.

Tomorrow could take care of itself. Tonight, she rested in the afterglow of what had been beautifully, undeniably real.

Chapter 31

I'll be there to pick you up at 9:30. Donovan's text from the night before sat at the top of Eden's phone when she woke up.

Eden smiled as she read it. She was genuinely looking forward to going to church with Donovan and his family, to stepping into something grounding during a season that'd stirred up so much movement in her life.

Her mother's voice surfaced gently in her mind.

Not every call is meant to be answered.

Eden wrapped herself in her robe and walked slowly through her home.

"*Why is Christopher reaching out to me now?* she wondered. *And do I even want to know?*"

Her phone buzzed again, then again. Notifications stacked quickly as the photos Krista posted continued to circulate. Likes multiplied. Comments piled on.

It was a lot.

Donovan would be there soon; she needed to hurry and get dressed.

Another message appeared.

Can't wait to see you. I'll be there in ten minutes.

Right on time, Donovan stood at her door.

"You ready?" he asked, his smile easy and reassuring.

"Yes," she said.

He offered his hand, palm up, simple and sure, and she took it without hesitation.

The drive was short. The church came into view, brick worn smoothly by decades of prayers. Cars fill the parking lot. And families streamed toward the entrance, bundled in coats and expectations.

As Donovan parked, he turned to her with a soft grin. "It's that time again. Gifting time."

She laughed lightly. "Of course it is."

"Today's theme is Return to intimacy with God," he said. The assignment is simple. Spend time in prayer or worship with no agenda."

Shaking her head in disbelief, she said, "How funny is it that's today's theme and we're literally about to walk into the church now. You have planned these days out like nobody's business."

He handed her a small bundle. "Here's your gift."

An elegant set of prayer cards, tied neatly with ribbon. Each card inscribed with a short prompt or verse, with space for reflection.

"Thank you." She leaned in, resting her forehead against his in a quiet, shared moment of devotion before they stepped out into the cold.

The December sun sparkled on the frost as they walked up to meet the family, hands intertwined and hearts open.

Donovan's mother stood just outside the entrance, dressed impeccably in a deep cranberry suit, pearls resting at her neck, and her Bible tucked under her arm. She gathered her family together before entering the sanctuary.

"This family goes to church together," she said plainly. "This is how we start Christmas week. As a family."

No one questioned it.

The entire family followed the matriarch and patriarch into the church.

Krista and Daniel trailed closely behind Donovan and Eden, playful whispers and laughter trailing close. Even Daniel, who admitted he hadn't been to church in a while, seemed surprisingly at ease.

Evergreen garlands framed the doors. White poinsettias surrounded the pulpit. Candles flickered softly along the aisle.

The choir stood dressed in freshly pressed robes and hit the first note of "Oh Come All Ye Faithful."

The sound filled the room, rich and full. The congregation stood as one. Eden felt it immediately, that rare thing when heaven and earth seem to agree with each other in your heart.

Donovan's mother sang every word without looking at the hymnal.

When the pastor stepped forward, his presence commanded attention without effort.

"You all may be seated," he said.

A gentle hush followed as everyone settled.

"Today," he began, "we're going to talk about the part of Christmas no one puts on a greeting card."

A ripple of knowing laughter moved through the room.

"The rumors. The raised eyebrows. The whispers behind hands. Mary wasn't celebrated. She was questioned. Joseph wasn't praised. He was doubted. And our Lord and Savior, Jesus wasn't born into clarity. No, He was born into controversy. He entered the world misunderstood."

The pastor opened his Bible.

"Let's start our text here at Matthew 1:19: *So her husband, Joseph, being a righteous man, and not wanting a disgrace her publicly, decided to divorce her secretly.*"

He adjusted his wireless microphone.

"Integrity. It can sometimes cost you your reputation before it rewards you with peace. Jesus wasn't born into applause. He was born into rumors, danger, and displacement. And while there were many stories told about them, they didn't stop their lives to correct everyone. They kept it moving."

Eden felt Donovan's thumb brush slow circles against her palm.

"Some of you," the pastor continued, "did the right thing and paid the wrong price for it. Unfortunately, you lost rooms you deserved to be in. Your opportunities dried up and people decided who you were without asking."

The words were finding agreement within the congregation.

"Amen," voices echoed through the congregation.

"But can I share something with you my brothers and sisters, "Heaven never misunderstood you."

Eden closed her eyes. This message wasn't coincidence. Mary, Joseph, and Jesus had each paid a tremendous cost. Eden wondered if the cost now pressing on her life would be worth it. Remaining where she was would be easier, safer.

"Now turn with me to Luke 2:7," he went on.

She wrapped him in clothes and placed him in a manger, because there was no guest room available for them.

"Some of you have shown up to places you were supposed to be and when you arrived, there was no room," he said.

"But just like God showed up for Mary, Joseph, and Jesus, He's going to show up for you too."

When service ended, Eden realized she held Donovan's hand the entire time.

Everyone walked out together feeling refreshed, renewed, and encouraged. Families hugged. People were heard shouting "Merry Christmas," across the parking lots like it was a blessing meant for everyone in earshot.

The Rivera family headed back to the house for Soulfood Sunday.

Fried chicken crackled. Collard greens simmered on low while the cornbread rested under a cloth. The macaroni and cheese and candied yams filled oversized aluminum pans, ready to be enjoyed.

Eden was welcomed again without needing to audition.

She left her phone on the table as she stepped away to use the restroom.

The screen lit up.

Christopher: *I miss you. I was hoping we could talk. Are you coming to meet me?*

Sitting next to Eden's phone, Krista saw it. Her face tightened.

When Eden returned, Krista didn't smile.

"Who's Christopher?" She asked, direct and sharp.

Eden didn't get defensive or over-explain. She met Krista's question calmly.

"He's someone I used to know but have no dealings with," she said simply.

Krista noticed Eden's restraint, and it only increased her respect for her.

That night, back home, the quiet returned.

Eden placed the prayer cards on the opposite nightstand, across from where Laurence's letter rested. She knelt beside her bed, not to ask for answers, but to give thanks.

Her phone buzzed again.

It was Christopher.

She chose not to respond. And not from avoidance but a discernment.

Instead, she whispered a prayer of gratitude. "Thank you, Lord."

She was grateful you could walk into a church holding the right hand and still have the past tapping your shoulder. And also grateful for who walked beside her into the sanctuary and never let go.

Chapter 32

Eden stepped through the entrance of the festival and slowed without meaning to. Thousands of lights draped the trees like jewelry, glowing as if they'd been waiting all year for this moment. Warm white bulbs blinked against the deep greens and silvery reflections. Nearby, a child squealed with delight. Farther off, a brass quartet warmed up, their instruments flashing under the lights as they worked through festive tunes.

Donovan walked beside her, their coats brushing as they moved. Their gloved hands found each other without formality, like something already agreed upon.

"Okay," Eden said, taking it all in. "Now this feels like a movie."

Donovan smiled. "You know you say that a lot."

"That's because my life has been aggressively cinematic here lately." She said, laughing.

He laughed too, low and easy, and she felt it in her chest more than she heard it.

They walked beneath a tunnel of lights that shifted from soft gold to pale blue. They passed families stopping for photos, couples laughing mid-spin. Children darted in and out holding glowing wands, chasing each other like they were made of starlight.

"Today's assignment," he said, as if continuing a conversation that started hours ago, "is presence."

She tilted her head toward him. "That's it?"

"That's it. No objects today. You are to choose someone you want to spend time with. Your presence is the present."

Eden slowed, then stopped completely.

He turned to face her. The lights behind him framed his silhouette.

"Well," she said, a small smile touching her mouth, "that part is easy."

Something in his expression was quietly pleased.

They resumed walking, slower now, passing a vendor pouring steaming cups of hot chocolate."

"Oh look," he said. "One of your favorites. I will get us a cup."

He stepped away and returned with two cups, handing her one.

Steam curled upward as she wrapped her hands around it.

"Oh my goodness," she said. "This is what I love about December."

He glanced at her. "The Hot chocolate?"

"Yes, but more than that." She gestured around them. "It's like everything slows down. People pay more attention and even joy feels deliberate."

"I think you're right", he said. "I think December tries to do that."

She smiled to herself, "That might be why I've never been too upset about being born in this month."

He looked over, teasing, "You have a birthday this month?"

"Mm-hmm."

In all the time they'd been spending together, anytime her birthday came close to the conversation, she'd gently redirected. This was the first time she'd brought it up on her own.

"Okay," he said, smiling. "I'm going to need more information, more details about this."

She laughed. "People have opinions about December birthdays, right? Half birthdays. Joint gifts. The whole 'this is for Christmas *and* your birthday' situation. I've always said if your birthday is before Christmas, you're lucky. It's those of us after the twenty-fifth who get the short end of the stick. By then, everyone's tapped out. Christmas is the star of the season."

Donovan winced. "That sounds rough."

Shrugging her shoulders, she said, "I think it taught me early how to share space. How to not take up too much of it. Or how to be grateful without asking for anything extra."

She took a sip of the hot chocolate, then added, "Or it teaches you to plan."

He smiled. "Oh," he said. "How Capricorn of you."

She laughed, surprised. "You know my sign?"

"I'm not into all of that but I know enough," he said. You don't miss details. You organize them. A textbook Capricorn."

They walked on, the path carving toward a lake where the lights reflected off the dark water, doubling themselves.

"I think December made me," she said after a moment. "Not just the birthday part. But the waiting and the expectation. It's like I know something is coming, but I'm learning not to rush it."

They walked in listening silence, a moment not asking to be filled.

As they passed under an archway of lights she spoke again. "There's something I want to share with you."

Without a word, Donovan guided them toward a quieter path, where the lights were lower, and a thinned crowd.

"A few years ago," she began, "there was a proposed partnership. Big money. Great press. You know, all the things. Everyone wanted to move fast."

She paused, choosing her words.

"I started noticing inconsistencies. Legal gray areas. The commas and the semicolons were telling me different stories.

"As an attorney," Donovan said lightly, "semicolons and commas, will always tell on people."

She smiled and then grew serious again. "Nothing was illegal on paper. But it was wrong in practice.

She swallowed.

"I raised concerns. I asked for more time. More transparency."

The lights caught in her eyes as she spoke.

"And that," she said quietly, "made me inconvenient. I was told, Eden you're overthinking this, we're risking momentum. They said I should just trust the process."

Pulling her coat tighter, "Little did they know, me and trust do not get along." She scoffed.

Donovan exhaled slowly.

"When I wouldn't sign off, the conversations changed. "Suddenly, I wasn't protecting integrity. I was difficult. Aggressive. Somehow, I became the liability."

She looked up at him.

"Nothing I did was improper. But perception has its own economy. Those types of rooms don't reward people who disrupt comfort, even when they're right. It's easier to sidestep the person asking the questions than to revisit what they exposed."

She paused briefly. "The board announcements are tomorrow. And with everything resurfacing...I don't know how everything is going to play out."

She waited. This was the first time she'd said it out loud to someone who wasn't already in her inner circle.

"That doesn't sound like a scandal to me," he said.

There was no shock in his voice.

His response wasn't what she imagined. "Did you know about this already?"

"I didn't know the details," he said honestly. "But I recognized the pattern. When someone *warns* you without facts or speaks around an issue instead of naming it, it's usually because the truth makes *them* uncomfortable."

"And you didn't say anything?"

"No," he said, stepping closer. "Because it didn't change how I see you. The way I see it, you refused to cross a boundary line."

Absorbing his words she said, "Speaking of boundary lines. There's more. I'm not sure if Krista mentioned something to you. But something happened yesterday and I want to be clear before anything gets misunderstood."

Eden released a slow breath.

"A text came through my phone and Krista saw it. Now, it could've been interpreted as something but it's not."

She tossed her empty cup into a nearby trash bin. "The timing of all of this is very loud."

Donovan listened.

"Anyway," she said circling back, "It was from someone I met recently. Someone who knew a version of me that doesn't exist anymore. Thanks to you and day twelve, I released that version."

"Eden, what you've described," he said, "isn't scandal or misunderstood text messages. It's courage that made people uncomfortable. I'm not afraid of that."

"Good. Because it seems to be following me these days."

"Then it follows me too."

They walked on, closer now, her arm tucked into his.

"You didn't have to tell me any of this," he said. "You choosing to share it matters. Not because I needed the information, but because you trust me with it."

She stopped and turned to him, taking both his hands in hers. "Today's assignment was presence," she said softly. "Choosing who to spend time with."

She squeezed his hands, making a bold declaration. "And Donovan. I choose you."

Through his gloved hands she could feel his thumb brush against her knuckles, steady and sure. "I know."

They continued down the illuminated path, the music swelling behind them, the lights stretched forward.

Their presence was the gift of the day. No wrapping. No announcement. Just two people walking side by side into whatever came next.

Chapter 33

"And why," Eden asked no one in particular, "did I think driving all the way out here was a *casual* Christmas errand?"

She was crammed into the backseat of Amara's SUV, wedged between gift bags and party supplies for Amara's Christmas Eve party. Traffic crawled along, thick with last-minute shoppers and blinking brake lights. The radio bounced between holiday songs and a cheerful voice reminding listeners not to leave valuables in plain sight.

Eden checked the address again, even though the navigation already announced they were near their destination.

"Because you're smitten," Katy said from the passenger seat, "and smitten people do ambitious things on Christmas Eve Eve."

Amara chimed in. "Also, because it's a great gift idea. I'm glad you saw the post online."

"It's been pretty hard not to see things online lately," Eden said, referring to her viral photo shoot. "But this is our first Christmas. I don't want to overdo it. I don't want to underdo it. I just want it to mean something."

Amara glanced at Eden through the rearview mirror. "Ma'am, you are attending an *auction* two days before Christmas for a *comic* book. I'd say meaning has arrived."

"Honey," Eden said, a little defensive, "this man takes out the trash without being asked. We are for sure hunting down this comic book."

Amara laughed. "I hear you girl. Men who take out the trash consistently do deserve respect."

Okay," Katy said, holding up a hand. "Before we step into rich people land and start bidding on paper that costs more than my first car, we need updates."

Amara nodded. "Yes. Catch us up."

Eden filled them in on the last few days.

Amara slowed at a red light. "Let's start with the pictures. Are we talking viral-viral or industry viral?"

"Industry," Eden said. "But close enough to the other that people from my past are crawling out of the woodwork like it's resurrection season. I thought it was Christmas, not Easter."

They turned onto a tree-lined street, the houses grew larger, set farther back from the road.

"And what about the board?" Amara asked.

"We find out today." Eden said.

Amara pulled into a long circular driveway framed by manicured hedges and an expansive lawn. She turned off the engine and looked back at Eden fully.

"And?"

"And, whatever happens," Eden said, "won't be the final word on my life."

The multi-car garage doors were opened revealing a small fleet of cars waiting to be auctioned.

"Hold on, wait." Katy said, unbuckling her seat belt. "I thought I was here to support you in your comic book adventure. I didn't realize I was also coming to buy a car."

She hopped out and added, "But first, let's go get your man a comic book."

Eden shook her head, grinning as she stepped out. "He's not my man."

Katy looped her arm through Eden's. "Yet."

Inside, the air smelled of old books and expensive artificial fragrances. They'd arrived just in time for the preview hour. Voices stayed low, measured. Even excitement behaved here.

They registered and wandered around.

Glass cases lined the walls. Paintings. Jewelry. Books with cracked spines and handwritten notes tucked between pages.

And then Eden saw it.

The comic book.

It sat alone, elevated, sleeved, and reverent. The colors were bold but softened with age.

"That's it," she whispered.

Katy squinted at the placard. "First edition. Original print. Authenticated."

Amara read the estimated value and let out a low whistle. "So... do we have a number where we physically retrain you?"

"Yes," Eden said smiling. "If I go over, stop me."

They laughed, easing closer as the auctioneer began, his voice smooth and practiced.

Eden watched the book like it might disappear if she blinked.

The bidding started.

Eden raised her paddle.

Someone across the room countered immediately.

All three whipped their heads around to see who the competition was.

"On no," Katy whispered. "They didn't come here to play. They came here to *win*. But so did we."

Eden raised the paddle again.

The numbers climbed. Her heart followed.

Her phone vibrated in her hand. Donovan's name lit the screen.

Thinking about you. I'll see you later.

She didn't look at it for long. She couldn't.

"Going once," the auctioneer said.

Eden held her breath.

"Going twice."

Katy crossed herself dramatically.

"Sold."

The gavel hit.

Eden froze.

Then Amara squeezed her hand. "You did it."

Katy jumped up clapping. "SHE DID THAT. NOW SOME-BODY GET THIS WOMAN SOME EGGNOG."

Eden laughed, stunned and glowing. "I can't believe I just did that."

Amara smiled. "I can. You're acting from love now. I'm proud of you. That was fun."

Katy nodded. "Same. And please never invite me to an auction ever again. I now need to call my insurance company and get a quote for my new imaginary car."

Chapter 34

C hristmas shopping two days before Christmas felt like a test of endurance and faith.

The mall was crowded, hands full of bags and store windows glowed like promises people were racing to keep. Eden and Donovan moved unhurried and out of step with the rush. Their calm pace almost felt rebellious.

They ducked into a small novelty shop tucked between two department stores. Eden drifted toward a display of ornaments while Donovan lingered near the counter.

When he came back, he was holding a rose gold karaoke microphone, sleek and unapologetically shiny.

She stared at it, then laughed. "You did not."

"I did," he said, pleased with himself. "Before you say anything, hear me out."

"I'm listening."

Today's theme is to restore your voice. The assignment... write a one-paragraph declaration of who you are becoming as you approach your birthday. Make it bold enough to give your younger self goose-bumps and then recite it in the microphone."

"This," he said, "felt like a reminder."

"A reminder of what?" she asked.

"That you don't need permission to be heard."

Before she could respond, both of their phones vibrated at the same time.

They looked at each other, neither reaching for a screen.

She turned the microphone in her hands, the metal cool against her fingers.

Eden felt it before she read a single word.

They walked past the extensive line of families waiting to take pictures with Santa and the smell of cinnamon pretzels lingering in the air.

"Let's sit for a minute," Donovan said. "Food court?"

She nodded.

They found an empty table tucked into a corner. Eden opened her email first.

The wording was careful, polite, and regretfully informing.

Nathanial had been successful.

The foundation had chosen to move forward with other candidates. They thanked her for her interest and acknowledged her contributions.

She let the words land without trying to reshape them into anything other than what it was.

Across from her, Donovan glanced at his phone, read quietly, then slipped it back into his pocket.

She met his eyes. "Did you get appointed?"

He shook his head once. "No."

"Oh no, I'm sorry Donovan. It looks like optics won. And you being seen with me cost you the appointment."

He reached across the table, taking her hand, "I'm not."

"You're not?"

"No," he said evenly. "And just so we're clear, I love being seen with you. If that disqualified me, then it wasn't a room I was meant to sit in. Plus, I sit on other boards."

For a moment, neither one of them spoke.

As if on cue, her phone buzzed again. This time it wasn't an email but a message request.

A woman she didn't know personally, but whose name she recognized immediately from a philanthropic storytelling panel she'd watched months earlier.

I've been following your work and recent visibility. I would love to meet and talk soon.

She reached into the bag and pulled out the microphone, resting it in her lap.

Today's theme," she said slowly, "was restore your voice."

"And?" he asked.

"And I think I finally understand what that means."

She didn't turn the microphone on.

Instead, she opened the notes app on her phone. Her thumbs hovered for a moment, then began to move. The words came steady. Her declaration was clear and unapologetic.

Donovan stood and said, "I'm going to give you a few minutes," he said. "I'll be back."

When she finished, she locked her phone and looked up at the ceiling lights glowing like constellations.

Donovan returned just as she lowered her gaze.

"All done?"

"Yes," she said. "I used to think being chosen was the evidence. Now I think being called is."

He smiled, small and certain.

They sat there a while longer, the mall moving around them, December alive and loud and generous, while something more solid took shape between them.

Chapter 35

Amara and Grant's house was already jumping before Eden even rang the bell.

Christmas lights spilled through the windows, casting flickering shadows over garland, stockings, and at least one inflatable reindeer that looked like it had opinions. Music thumped from inside; the unmistakable sound of Christmas joy mixed with full-bodied commotion.

Someone was laughing hard.

Someone else was absolutely singing off-key.

"Are you ready for this?" Eden asked, her hand hovering near the doorbell.

"I'm ready if you are." Donovan said.

The door swung open before she could press it.

"HO HO HO AND MERRY CHRISTMAS," Amara announced, wearing an ugly Christmas sweater she clearly made herself, blinking aggressively as if it demanded attention.

Grant appeared behind her holding a tray of drinks. "Coats to the left, dignity to the right." Both are optional."

The house smelled like cinnamon, toasted marshmallows, and something fried that definitely didn't come from a recipe blog.

A fire crackled in the backyard fire pit, where people were already attempting s'mores with mixed success.

Katy and Marcel were near the tree, deep in an argument over which classic Christmas song was objectively the best.

"Before I forget," Eden said to Amara, "I mentioned the party to Krista. Would you mind if she and Daniel came by?"

Amara didn't hesitate. "Of course. The more the merrier."

"Perfect," Eden said. "I'll text her."

When Krista and Daniel arrived, Krista wore a sweater so over-the-top festive it felt intentional. Daniel followed with a bottle of wine and the wide-eyed look of someone stepping into an extremely specific group of friends for the first time.

Within minutes, they were fully initiated.

Ugly sweater judging happened immediately and unfairly.

Grant clinked a spoon against his glass. "Alright, people. We're moving into Karaoke: Christmas Edition. No talent required."

Someone attempted, *All I Want for Christmas Is You* and had to restart twice. Someone else committed fully to *This Christmas* and received a standing ovation they absolutely didn't earn.

Donovan was laughing, loud, and unguarded. He lost a game and didn't argue the rules. He sang karaoke terribly and burned a marshmallow and ate it anyway.

Krista noticed.

Not in a dramatic way. Not all at once. Just in the quiet inventory a daughter takes without meaning to.

Daniel leaned toward her and whispered, "Your dad's fun."

"Yeah. He is."

Out back, the fire pit had become the center of gravity. People hovered with skewers and paper plates, debating the correct marshmallow-to-chocolate ratio like it was constitutional law.

Later, during the White Elephant Gift Exchange, craziness reached its peak.

Someone stole a candle three times. Someone else ended up with sock that read, *Jesus Is the Reason* on one foot and *For the Season* on the other. Grant pretended to cry when his gift was taken. Amara declared new rules mid-round that benefited her exclusively. Because Amara always won a game, even when she lost.

Eden laughed until her jaws were sore.

At one point, someone asked about her birthday.

"So, what are we doing" Katy asked casually, sipping her drink.

Eden looked around the room. At the firepit. The laughter. The people she loved gathered without effort.

"I want this," she said simply. "I want to be surrounded by people I love."

Donovan squeezed her hand.

Later, when the night slowed and people gathered in smaller circles, Eden slipped onto the couch by Donovan.

Eden watched Grant pull Amara into a dance together, despite her protests about the playlist. Twenty-nine years together and he still looked at her like she'd hung the moon. Eden wanted that. The certainty.

Donovan put one of his arms around her. He called for Amara.

"Hey Amara, do you have that pack of index cards I gave you to hold for me?" He asked.

Amara passed the packet of small blank index cards to Eden like a party favor.

"Here you go ma'am."

"Thank you, Amara." Donovan said.

"This is your gift for the day my lady."

"Index cards?" Eden said laughing.

"Yes, index cards. Do you want to know the theme for today?"

"Of course I do. I need to see how the index cards come into play."
She said, smiling.

"The theme is dream the impossible dream. Your assignment: the
unreasonable list. Write fifty things you want that feel somewhat unreasonable. Not impossible but just slightly out of reach."

"Oh, I like it. I can do that. I'll work on this later tonight. Thank
you." She said.

Donovan leaned over. "No pressure."

She smiled and said, "I kind of like the pressure."

Across the room, Krista watched her father with Eden.

This was new. And she approved.

Inside, the night wound down in pieces. Coats were gathered. Left-
over desserts were packed up. Hugs lingered.

Krista hugged Eden before leaving. "Thank you for inviting us,
tonight was fun. Merry Christmas Eden."

"Merry Christmas Krista."

Krista hugged Donovan and whispered, "You look...happy."

He glanced at her, then smiled. "I am."

Christmas Eve had done what it always does best.

When Eden returned home, she reached for the stack of index cards.
She started writing her list and was reminded that joy didn't have to be
loud to be real. That laughter could heal without announcing itself.

And sometimes, the most unreasonable dream of all was believing
you were allowed to want more.

Chapter 36

Eden woke before the sun, the way she always did when she slept at her parents' home.

There were no sirens, no overhead neighbors pacing the floor. Just the soft tick of the hallway clock and the wind moving gently through the bare winter branches outside her window.

Coming there the night before felt sudden but right. After Amara's party, after the laughter and full joy of it all, she didn't want to stay in the city. She decided to wake up somewhere that held her history.

Staring at the ceiling of her childhood bedroom, she let herself remember how many Christmas mornings had started exactly like this.

Eden had siblings, of course. They were simply scattered now, busy with families of their own, lives that pulled them in different directions. She had always been the one closest to home, the one who stayed.

Down the hall, a floorboard creaked.

Liora.

Eden smiled at the familiar sound.

She rose slowly, wrapping herself in her robe, savoring the stillness before the day's celebrations.

The house was already warm when she reached the kitchen.

Her mother stood at the counter in her own robe, hair wrapped and moving with Christmas morning purpose.

The coffee pot gurgled as if it had something special to say. The bacon sizzled while the eggs fluffed. Hash brown crisped up in a pan. Chocolate croissants warmed in the oven, a Liora Christmas tradition that had never once been questioned.

Her father sat at the table, glasses low on his nose, reading something in the newspaper, a ritual done more out of habit than necessity.

"Well," her mother said, turning towards Eden. "Merry Christmas."

"Merry Christmas," Eden replied, stepping easily into the hug that had been waiting for her.

Her father stood to kiss her on the cheek and squeeze her shoulder twice. Their old, quiet language.

Christmas classics played in the background of their morning. Their breakfast together was slow. Their conversations wandered from hither to yon. Stories that'd been told before but were never tired of being heard.

"Eden, baby," her father said after a moment, folding the paper. "Have you heard yet?"

"Heard what, Daddy?"

"Marvin Coleson passed last night."

Eden's breath hitched. "Oh no, on Christmas Eve? No, I hadn't heard that yet."

"Yeah, we got word early this morning. They say they are going to bury him this Saturday." Liora said.

Marvin Coleson. A giant in their political world. A man who'd touched and impacted many lives.

Eden looked at both her parents with a quiet reflection, she was grateful to still have them both in her life.

Midway through breakfast, Liora reached across the table and rested her hand over Eden's.

"You look good baby," she said. "You look rested. You look...free."

Eden considered her mother's words.

"I'd have to say the same baby girl. I agree with your mother." Her father replied.

"That's because I am."

Her father nodded, as if that explained everything.

The morning stretched open from there. They moved into the family room where the Christmas tree stood full and familiar. The ornaments told the family story if you knew how to read them. Her siblings' childhood crafts. Her nephew's handprint from a few years back. Evidence that life kept expanding, even when everyone wasn't in the same room anymore.

They exchanged a few gifts by the fire.

The laughter, the love, the life they shared in that moment was the greatest gift for all of them.

Eden was used to rushing through mornings.

Today, she didn't.

She listened more than she talked, absorbing nuggets of wisdom shared by her parents. She laughed without checking the time. She let herself be a daughter, not the strong one holding the room together and fixing things.

Later, bundled in coats, they took a short walk down the road. The fields were pale and still, the air sharp and clean. Eden breathed deeply, thinking about how much had changed over the last month.

By late afternoon, she was preparing to head out for the evening.

Liora hugged her longer than usual. "Have a good evening," she said. "And tell Donovan we said Merry Christmas."

Her father squeezed her hand. "Drive safe. And tell that Donovan, I am ready for that Spades game, whenever he is."

Eden laughed. "I'll be sure to tell him. I'll see you guys when I get back."

The drive back to the city felt different than the one the night before.

Anticipatory.

Tonight, would be her first time at Donovan's home.

Dusk had settled in by the time she arrived.

He opened the door with his sleeves rolled up, an apron tied around his waist, the scent of roasted garlic and citrus drifted out ahead of him.

"Merry Christmas," he said.

"Merry Christmas," she replied, stepping inside as he kissed her softly.

His home felt like him. Calm and considered. Clean without being staged. His books, arranged by use, not color. Art chosen carefully. A life lived thoughtfully.

Inside his kitchen, he'd started their prep work, which was simmering and roasting when she arrived. They cooked together, learning the choreography of sharing his kitchen.

Handing her a glass a wine, he asked, "So, how was the first part of your day?"

"It was great," she said. I love being out there with them."

"I can see why. It's very nice out there."

She smiled. "Well, it looks like you're going out there soon. My dad told me to tell you he's ready for that card game you promised."

"That's my guy. I'll make it happen."

The dinner prepared by their own hands was eaten by candlelight, laughter slipping in between bites.

"Hey, did you hear about Marvin?" She asked as they cleared the dishes and made their way into the living room.

"Yes, I did. I saw the statement his family put out on social media earlier. Looks like I'll be going to a funeral this weekend." He said.

"Yeah, you and me both. We should definitely go together."

"I agree," he said but his agreement carried more than logistics.

"Here," he said handing her a box, "I have something for you."

She smiled and said looking around, "I have something for you too. How are we going to do this?"

"Let's just grab everything and sit here." He said gathering their things together.

They sat close, knees nearly touching.

He went first.

He handed her the first box again and then another box.

Inside the first box was a watch. Her favorite brand.

She gasped, "No, you did not!"

"Oh, yes I did!"

At an earlier meeting, Donovan noticed she didn't wear a watch. In a passing conversation, he asked Katy about it and she shared someone had stolen her other one and Eden hadn't gotten around to replacing it.

Lifting him in a hug, she laughed overwhelmed, "Why are you like this?"

"Hmm, I'm not really sure how to answer that." He said, handing her the second box.

Eden opened it to find delicate charms, journal charms, small and meaningful.

"Today's theme," he said gently scootching in closer to her, "is Renew Your Habits.

Eden sat listening.

"Take one old habit," he said continuing. "Replace it with a new one that matches your next chapter. You already journal. Think of these charms as reminders. They're like journal jewelry or something like that. You'll use these as little celebrations of the habits you want to keep."

She leaned in and kissed him. "I already know of one habit I want to keep."

Then it was his turn.

Eden hopped up from the floor and reached for Donovan's gift.

Eden watched his face change in real time.

He tore away the paper and stopped.

"Oh no you didn't!" He said, breathless.

"Oh yes I did!" She teased.

The comic book sat framed like art. Because it was.

He laughed once, shook his head, and said, "Yes, you really did."

He looked at her, leaned in, hugging her like the world narrowed to just the two of them, careful not to crush the gift, careful not to speak until he'd fully absorbed the moment.

"This is...incredible and I know the perfect place to hang it. How did you know?"

Before she could answer, her phone buzzed violently on the table.

Katy's face filled the screen.

Glancing down, she laughed. "Oh no."

Answering, Katy's eyes widened, her voice halfway to shouting and jumping up and down. Marcel stood beside her, grinning.

"EDEN," Katy yelled. "HE GOT IT."

"Got what?" Eden squinted.

Eden turned the camera front facing.

"THE CAR," Katy screamed. "FROM THE AUCTION. OH MY GOD, I CAN BARELY BREATHE!"

Marcel leaned into the frame, "Merry Christmas guys."

Eden clapped her hand over her mouth, laughing. "Oh my goodness; I'm so happy for your Katy. Merry Christmas guys."

As the on-screen celebration continued, Donovan glanced at her.

When the call ended, he nodded toward the phone.

"He told me he was going to do it," Donovan said casually. Then, after a beat, he said, "I guess some people just decide someone's worth the effort."

She met his eyes. She understood. That was his way of letting her know he knew the lengths she'd gone through to get the comic book.

Later, they sat together, quiet but connected.

When Eden rested her head against his shoulder, it felt less like a habit and more like learning something she wanted to remember.

Not every habit needed to be broken. Some were worth choosing. Choosing what nourished rather than numbed. That insight unwrapped like a small Christmas miracle.

Chapter 37

Katy and Amara waited in the driveway of Eden's parents' home, the engine idling, holiday music playing a touch too loud.

When Eden finally stepped outside, bundled in a thick coat with a matching scarf, hat, and mittens, shopping bags swinging at her side, Katy let out a squeal.

"You like it?" Katy asked, bouncing in the driver's seat.

Eden opened the back door and climbed in. "It's a car, Katy. But yes, I like it. And the fact you drove all the way out here to pick me up tells me you really love it."

"Girl, love is an understatement." Amara said, twisting around in her seat. "She's been explaining every feature to me since we left my house."

"I'm sorry. I can't help it," Katy said, grinning wide as she pulled onto the road. "I absolutely love this car and the man who gave it to me."

"Well good," Eden said, laughing as the car picked up speed. "All that love saved me a drive into the city. I'm truly happy for you Katy."

Katy's enthusiasm carried them down the highway faster than the law allowed but her joy was nearly infectious. By the time they pulled into the mall parking lot, Eden and Amara had loosened into laughter and caught up to Katy's energy.

Inside, the mall buzzed with post-holiday hysteria. Shoppers moved in every direction, arms full of bags, voices raised, gift cards burning holes in pockets. Some negotiated returns with tired clerks. Others clutched new purchases like victories.

A display of discounted snow globes nearly met its end when Katy misjudged a turn and Amara mumbled under her breath about the crowds and her rapidly thinning patience.

Eden drifted between them, somewhere between observation and amusement, letting both their moments play out.

They moved in and out of stores, each with a few items to return or exchange.

"So," Amara said, leaning in with a smile that was playful but direct, "it sounds like you and Donovan had a great Christmas. How are things going with him? And be honest. Did you get a boyfriend for Christmas?"

Eden paused, running her fingers over a sweater on a rack. "We had a great Christmas, it was a beautiful day," she said. "Starting with my parents. Staying out there reminds me to settle myself." She smiled faintly. "And the evening with Donovan was delightful. I don't think I got a boyfriend for Christmas, but we definitely have something. And I'm okay not naming it yet."

Amara nodded, then sharpened her focus. "Okay, that's Donovan. Any news on Christopher?"

Eden's smile was quiet but firm. "No news is good news. He stopped reaching out. I think he got the hint because no response is still a response."

Katy slowed to a stop, shifting her weight, her smile turning unsure. "I hope you won't get upset but I should tell you something. A couple of weeks ago, he stopped me outside of our building. He said he was trying to get in touch with you. He wanted to get you something for Christmas and your birthday. I told him I couldn't help him."

Eden reached out, resting her hand briefly on Katy's arm. "Listen, you don't have to be afraid to tell me things. And honestly, it wouldn't have mattered. He made his choice. I made mine."

Amara raised her eyebrow, teasing. "Hmm. You've made a choice, huh? So you *did* get a boyfriend for Christmas?

They started walking again.

Eden gestured around them, palms out, as if addressing an invisible audience. "No. And at this big age, do we even ask someone to be a girlfriend or boyfriend? Do we send a...calendar invite?"

There was a beat of silence before all three of them burst into laughter, the absurdity of middle-aged adult dating expectations settling over them like a shared inside joke.

Eden glanced down at her phone. A missed call from Donovan followed by a text.

"Hey Katy," she said looking up. "When we leave here, can you drop me off at my place? Donovan wants to meet me there. He has something for me, and then he'll take me back to my parents."

"Donovan, Donovan," Amara teased. "If you didn't get a boyfriend at Christmas. Maybe you'll get him for your birthday."

"He's definitely Birthday-Bae," Katy added.

They linked arms as they walked out of the mall, laughter following them into the cold air.

Later that afternoon, Eden set her bags down at home and freshened up, smoothing her sweater and checking the mirror just as the doorbell rang.

When she opened the door, Donovan stood there holding boxes and storage bags, stacked carefully in his arms.

She opened the door and he stood with boxes and storage bags.

She blinked. "What is all this?"

"Hi," he said, smiling with mischief. "This is your gift for today."

She stepped aside, widening the door to let him in.

"I heard you were in town," he continued as he set everything down. "And Katy is...extremely excited about the car, huh?"

"Overjoyed," Eden confirmed.

"So," Donovan said, straightening up, "today's theme is actually perfect, considering what you all did at the mall. Returning and exchanging."

He handed her a small satin pouch.

Eden peeked inside. A small coin flashed in the light, stamped with a single word: **Keep**.

Flipping the coin over in her hand. "This is cute," she said. "But what am I supposed to keep?"

"Only what you choose," she said. The boxes and bags are because I came to help you sort. Clothes too worn, too small, or too tied to old stories. What doesn't stay gets donated or tossed. I did this recently myself. It's very freeing. Also," he added, "a nice tax deduction."

Eden laughed. "So, this is adulting. Sorting through old jeans for emotional clarity and tax purposes."

They spent the next several hours talking and laughing, sitting on the floor as piles formed around them. They talked about life, current projects, hopes for the year ahead and what that might look like for them.

When the last bag was sealed, Donovan glanced at her. There's only a few more days until your birthday and I wanted to let you know we've all been planning something. I know you don't love surprises, so I wanted to be upfront."

Eden smiled. "Do I get to know what we're doing?"

"You'll find out on your birthday."

She looked around the room, the piles neatly organized. "Wow. You don't realize how much you accumulate over the years. Thank you."

"Of course," he said, smiling.

The holiday magic lingered. Not in carols or decorations, but in quiet acts of love, friendship, and choice.

Eden was keeping what mattered.

Chapter 38

The church was already full when Donovan and Eden arrived.

They paused at the top of the steps, not out of hesitation, but instinct. Some rooms announced themselves before you enter them. This was one of those rooms.

Eden had chosen black, simple, and structured, softened by a coat that had seen her through enough seasons to feel trustworthy. Donovan had chosen the same restraint. Together, they looked inevitable.

The service was held downtown, in a space designed for reverence without religion. A room meant to honor legacy.

Her parents had decided to live stream the service and watch it at home. Grief, they'd learned, did not require proximity to be sincere.

Marvin would have appreciated the turnout. Not for the numbers, but for the range.

Board members sat beside interns. Donors besides artists. Old power beside emerging vision. This, Eden realized, was Marvin's final lesson. A well-lived life made room for everyone.

The quartet entered the sanctuary together.

Not intentionally but they moved as one body, without trying, drawing attention without demanding it. Heads turned and whispers followed. No one could quite name what they were sensing, only that something about seeing them together felt like a preview.

They didn't know it yet but by the time the industry caught up, this moment would be replayed in hindsight. People would say, *we should have known then*.

Clusters of people gathered before the memorial began, greeting one another in low voices.

The philanthropic media storyteller spotted Eden almost immediately. She crossed the room with the ease of someone who understood divine timing and momentum.

"Eden," she said warmly, shaking hands all around. "I'm so glad you're here. Marvin mattered. But so does who is standing here now."

Eden nodded. "Marvin lived like he expected the future to show up."

The woman smiled, the way people do when they recognize their own language being spoken fluently. "Exactly. And that's rare. But that's what I see in you, too. You're going to change things. People won't know how it happened. They'll just wake up one day and realize the story sounds different."

Eden didn't deflect. She simply said, "Thank you. We're going to take our seats now, but we'll talk soon."

At the front of the room, Marvin's portrait smiled the way it always had. The expression of a man who had seen ambition up close and survived it without being cruel.

Nearby, the foundation founders stood together, somber, and reflective. They were not villains. Just people who had learned to confuse fear with responsibility. Pressure had taught them to protect systems instead of souls.

Their eyes drifted, repeatedly, toward Donovan and Eden. Toward the space between them and the confidence around them. Their magnetism was undeniable, and it stung in the precise place it was meant to.

Nathaniel lingered in the perimeter.

He watched Eden the way threatened men do, with calculation disguised as detachment. His eyes never stopped moving. This was a room where influence was shifting and he could feel it in his bones.

Donovan's hand found the small of Eden's back like a magnet, guiding her into the pew where four seats were still available.

The service started right on time.

Stories were shared. Marvin was spoken of as a builder, yes, but more than that, a releaser. Someone who believed leadership was proven by what continued without you. Someone who made space, deliberately.

There was no formal eulogy. The stories themselves became the sermon.

Fifty years of service. Marvin's life stood as a rebuke to the myth that power must corrupt. He proved legacy could move without being threatened. That chains don't need to be broken if they're fastened correctly in the first place.

Eden thought about Laurence and then Jubilee. Not the word but the order of it. There's release, then return, and restoration.

Around her, others were taking inventory, just as she was. Of what they'd built. Of who they'd withheld. Of who'd they delayed.

Nathaniel shifted in his seat.

When the service ended, the room didn't rush to empty. Conversations lingered. Connections reoriented. Futures adjusted themselves subtly.

Eden stood beside Donovan, watching it all.

Donovan watched too. He understood rooms like this. He also understood funerals were not about grief but redistribution.

This wasn't an ending or a farewell. It was an initiation.

Nathaniel locked in on Eden. He'd been watching her the entire service. As they were leaving, he realized he was about to miss his big opportunity.

"Hey Eden. I see you've been getting a lot of attention lately," he said. "Visibility can be... unpredictable. It changes how people are perceived. And, of course, you were very close with the nomination. That kind of near-miss can be..." He let the thought hang, unfinished, a polite edge to his words.

Eden offered a calm, controlled smile. "Thank you, I appreciate your concern, enjoy the rest of your day," she said evenly, her tone courteous but firm, giving him nothing to press.

On their way out of the sanctuary she turned to Donovan, a smirk showed up. "I guess he thought he did something right there. Sometimes the best response to small men is to simply outgrow them," she said smiling.

Donovan raised an eyebrow, a quiet chuckle escaping him, and she leaned slightly into his side, savoring the private moment of shared amusement.

Back in his car, on the way to the repast, Donovan reached into the center console and pulled out a small bag.

Tipping the bag over into her hand, a single chain link dropped into the palm of her hand.

"I couldn't have planned today's gift better if I tried," he said. "Marvin's service paired perfectly.

"Is this a new style of jewelry?" Eden asked.

"It's not," Donovan said, glancing at her, then back at the road.

"Marvin understood release by right," he said. "Succession isn't about waiting until someone's ready. It's about knowing when a season has legally ended. Some things don't belong to us anymore. Not because we failed, but because time itself has moved on."

Eden rolled the chain between her fingers.

"Chains hold systems together," he said. "Industries. Boards. Gatekeepers. Power structures. They decide who's connected and who isn't."

"So why give me a chain?" she asked.

"Because you're not meant to carry the whole chain," he said gently. "You're meant to become a new connection point."

Eden leaned back against the seat thinking.

"*This*, this is Jubilee," he added. "Restoration in the truest sense. What no longer has authority over you gets released."

Eden thought back on the boardrooms that never quite opened. The ways some people still spoke to her as if she was *almost* ready.

"So, what's the assignment?" she asked.

Donovan smiled. Just enough.

"Choose one thing," he said. "One role, one rule, or relationship you've been honoring past its expiration date and let it go. Release it."

She nodded.

"I already know what it is," she said.

"I figured you would. And this release will be perfect for our date tomorrow."

They drove the rest of the way to the repass in silence.

Eden closed her fingers around the chain link.

She wasn't breaking anything. She was releasing it.

Somewhere between the funeral and the repast, Jubilee did what it always does.

It restored what had always been hers.

Chapter 39

Brunch wasn't necessarily planned, but Donovan knew it was Eden's favorite meal. That knowledge made his choice for the restaurant, deliberate. A quiet way to honor her as the days ticked closer to her birthday.

Eden slipped her coat off and slid next to Donovan, noticing how easy it felt to sit there with him.

"You look happy," he said, watching her over his coffee.

"I feel...the only way I can describe as, supercalifragilisticexpiali-docious,' she admitted grinning. "New language for me, but here we are."

He smiled, pleased with joy. The unspeakable kind.

They shared plates. Stolen bites and kisses. They leaned in talking like the world wasn't listening. Their knees brushed under the table and neither of them moved away.

After brunch, they walked it off, hands brushing until they laced their fingers naturally.

"Where to?" she asked.

Tilting his head to a nearby rink, Donovan asked, "You trust me?"

She squeezed his hand. "Haven't I been doing that for weeks now?"

The ice rink buzzed with sound and motion. Laughter and music. The scrape of blades against ice. Eden hesitated for exactly half a second before stepping on, gripping the rail.

Donovan skated backward in front of her, arms out.

"Come on," he said. "I've got you."

"You say that like it's a guarantee."

"Because it is," he replied.

She pushed off, wobbling, laughing, clinging to him, and as promised, he caught her effortlessly. Their faces were close. Close enough to feel the warmth of each other's breath, they moved together, finding a rhythm that was theirs alone.

"You're doing great," he whispered.

And she was. Eden let herself lean into him, trusting their steps, their timing, the synchronicities that had grown between them over the weeks of laughter, lesson, and gifts. 7

They skated slowly at first, then faster, playful, falling once and laughing hard. By the time they stepped off the ice, flushed, and breathless, Eden knew.

Her rhythm.

They found a bench, shoulders touching, coats half-zipped, but the cold chill clung to them.

"That," she said, catching her breath, "was exactly what I needed."

"And that's today's theme."

She turned to him. "Oh?"

"Find your rhythm," he said. Not anyone else's. Yours."

"And the gift?" she teased.

He didn't answer right away.

Instead, he reached into his pocket and pulled out something slowly.

"I've had it for a while," he said. "It generally sits on my desk."

Eden cupped her hands to receive it.

"When things start feeling loud or rushed," he continued, "I flip it.
I don't make decisions until the sand finishes falling. I'm not chasing
time; I'm moving through it."

Eden flipped it once, watching the sand make its slow descent.

"I love this," she said softly.

He smiled. "I hoped you would."

They sat a while longer, letting the day stretch, letting their silence
speak.

Helping her slip her skates off, he said, "There's one more thing."

She pulled her foot free with a little flourish.

"Tomorrow's the last day before your birthday," he said. "The final
assignment."

She waited.

"How do you feel about a water fast? Just for the day. Nothing
extreme. Just a way to clear space before the big day. The big five-oh."

Eden didn't hesitate.

"Yes, she said. "Of course. At this point, why wouldn't I finish
strong?"

"I had a feeling you'd say yes," Donovan said with gentle eyes. "And
that's one of the things I love about you. Not because you always say
yes but because you don't start something unless you can finish it."

With these two, love didn't need to announce itself but somehow
it had and Eden heard it.

"And that's one of the things I love about you, too." She said,
letting her fingers touch his.

"Oh yeah, and what is that?"

"You're just you. You notice little things that make the big things matter. From start to finish, you see me."

But Donovan wasn't the only one who noticed her.

Christopher, in town briefly for the holidays, taking a stroll, spotted them. He saw her, saw Donovan with her, and in that instant, he realized he would never have his place in her life. Not in six months, not ever. He was too late. His love would have to find space elsewhere.

Somewhere between brunch and ice, Eden realized a simple truth: she wasn't preparing for her birthday anymore.

She was preparing for Jubilee.

Chapter 40

Eden woke up once again at her parents' home. This would be the last day here before returning to the city tomorrow.

She rose slowly, letting the morning open up around her. There was no rush, no urgent demands. Just a day of gentle pausing, inviting her to step fully into herself. She moved to the kitchen for her first glass of lemon-infused water. The aroma of coffee and freshly baked bread teased her senses, but she let it pass, savoring stillness instead.

Settling by the window, she watched the frost trace delicate patterns across the garden. Her mind was full, carrying the weight of the past twenty-seven days. Each day, each small gift, each nudge had led her here.

She closed her eyes, inhaling deeply. Each breath was cleansing, each exhale was a surrender. Gratitude rose in her. Grateful for Donovan, her parents, her friends, and the unexpected joy tucked into the corners of her life.

Laurence's words echoed in her heart.

Her phone, set to Do Not Disturb, chimed gently. Donovan sent her a carefully curated playlist titled, "*27 Days of You*," with a note: For reflection, clarity, and your next chapter.

She pressed play. The first song was soft, meditative, notes stretching like sunlight across the room. She let the music guide her thoughts, each track evoking memories and feelings.

She thought of the laughter with Amara and Grant, of the quiet encouragement from her parents, of Donovan's thoughtfulness woven into each gift. Every track felt like a small act of blessing her past, present, and future.

By mid-morning, Eden was sitting in the family room, knees drawn to her chest, her journal open but untouched. The playlist played beside her, a soundtrack for reflection. She focused on her heart, on the choices she wanted to carry forward, the habits she intended to keep, the love she would continue to nurture. Her mind was clear, her intentions deliberate.

This wasn't a mid-life crisis. This was mid-life clarification. She smiled at the realization.

She paused for prayer, whispering gratitude and hope. Today's fast wasn't about deprivation; it was more about creating space for God's guidance. Each sip of water, each moment of stillness, cleared more than just her body. It cleared her mind and heart.

As the afternoon waned, she stretched her arms, feeling centered and ready. Tomorrow, her birthday would arrive, but today she was preparing the ground. She had cleared, reflected, released, and received.

Her eyes glanced at her journal, remembering Donovan's charms, the sand timer, the framed comic book. All the tokens of the journey she had been living. Each a reminder of the life she was choosing.

Closing her journal, Eden whispered a quiet thanks. To God, to Donovan, to herself. She could feel the presence of love guiding her, invisible hands interwoven into each day, each moment, each revelation.

She was ready. One hundred percent ready.

Chapter 41

Eden woke up before her alarm, not startled but aware. She understood the miracle immediately.

She was here.

Alive. Well. Fifty. Golden.

God had kept her.

The number didn't scare her. It didn't feel heavy or sharp the way she'd once imagined, it felt earned. Like a crown you don't rush to pick up until your neck is strong enough to carry it.

She lay still for a moment, hand resting over her heart, and whispered a simple thank you. Not for getting older, but wiser. From her bag, she pulled Laurence's letter and read it again, this time, choosing to fully step into her Jubilee.

But what had it cost her to take that step? The old self had to be released so the next chapter could be lived by right, who she actually was now. Change does cost but in this case it was worth it.

Down the hall, the house stirred.

Her parents were already up, pretending they weren't trying to be quiet.

When Eden stepped into the kitchen, balloons and streamers filled the kitchen.

Her mother turned, as if she'd been up all night waiting to say, "Merry Birthday," pulling Eden into a hug layered with decades of love.

Her father followed, kissing her temple. "Happy Birthday, kid. Fifty looks good on you."

Breakfast was gentle. Fresh fruit and warm tea, to honor her fast and body. They didn't overwhelm her stories or speeches. They just let her be. The time for that would come later. They knew well enough to understand this morning belonged to her spirit before it belonged to celebration.

Afterward, Eden dressed slowly, choosing clothes that felt like herself, not behind a mask of who she thought she should be at fifty.

She paused in front of the mirror, studying the reflection that stared back. For a moment, she barely recognized the woman smiling back at her.

Who is this woman who laughs this freely now?

Her phone buzzed breaking into her thoughts.

A message from Donovan.

Happy Birthday, baby. Looking forward to celebrating you later.

Messages from her siblings rolled in throughout the morning, full of love, voice notes, and inside jokes that didn't need explaining.

By late afternoon, she arrived at the location she'd been told to come without asking too many questions. It wasn't a restaurant. It wasn't a ballroom. It was a restored historic space tucked just outside the city, wrapped in elegance.

As soon as she stepped inside, the room unfolded.

Candles. Soft music. A long table dressed in linen and greenery, set not for spectacle but for communion.

Her people stood there, all of them, waiting.

Her parents.

Amara and Grant.

Katy and Marcel, holding hands.

Krista and Daniel, her eyes already misted.

And Donovan.

He stood slightly apart, with long-stemmed roses in hand.

For a moment, Eden couldn't move.

It wasn't the setup that left her undone. It was the intention. Every detail said, *we see you. We know you. We honor who you've become.*

Applause broke the spell, with laughter following closely behind. Hugs came in waves. Long ones. Tight ones.

Krista hugged her last, handing Eden a framed photo from their shoot.

Eden felt the weight of the gesture before she opened it. Their relationship had found its own footing. Krista wasn't standing there as an extension of her father. She was standing there on her own, as Eden's friend.

Dinner stretched out like a love letter. Stories were shared. Toasts were lifted. Amara made everyone laugh until they cried. Grant spoke about timing and legacy. Katy squeezed Eden's hand like she was holding a secret.

Amara raised her glass first, eyes glistening. "Eden, it's beautiful to finally see you this way, she said, her voice soft but steady. "Like the world's been waiting for this version of you, and now it's here."

Katy laughed, clinking her glass lightly against Eden's. "Well, I always knew you were a little unstoppable," she said. "But you now look like you are about to be an entire problem for some folks. Happy Birthday Eden."

Marcel kept looking at Katy like a man on the edge of doing something wonderful. He had *that* look.

Krista's eyes held quiet reverence. "Eden, life rewards those who step fully into their own light. I've seen you do that," she said, her words carrying a gentle conviction. "Never dim it for anyone, not for a single minute of your life."

Finally, Donovan reached for her hand, holding it as if it always belonged there. His eyes searched hers, steady and unwavering.

"And through it all," he said, his voice low and intimate, "I see you. Every hope, every strength, every part of you I get to love. Today, tomorrow, and all the days beyond. You are everything I've been waiting for. Happy Birthday my love."

Then Eden's father stood.

The room quieted.

He did not speak long. He never did.

"Fifty," he said, "is not about what you have accumulated. It is about what you're trusted with."

He handed her an envelope.

Inside was a commitment. A financial gift from John and Liora and Laurence and Millie, prayed over and placed with intention. This gift was not for indulgence but for impact.

"For Jubilee," he said. "For what you're building next."

Eden sat back slowly, emotions pressing into her chest. This wasn't money. This was a permission slip. This was partnership.

Krista slipped away quietly at some point, phone in hand.

She had a way of doing that.

Later, as dessert was served and the room softened, Donovan reached for Eden's hand.

"There's one last thing," he said.

They stepped aside, just enough to create a pocket of privacy inside the room.

"The twenty-seven days are complete," Eden said softly. "Which means I have to ask."

He smiled, already knowing.

"How'd you do it?" she asked. "All the gifts. The assignments. How'd you come up with all of that?"

Donovan took a breath.

"Now remember Katy jump started this. However, I was able to do it because someone once did it for me," he said. "Before my fiftieth, I was at a low point. I didn't trust myself with what might lie ahead. They saw something in me, I couldn't quite see yet."

He met her eyes.

"I worked through my worst so I could be ready to give you, my best. Loving you isn't accidental. I prepared for you."

Even though the party was her gift, Donovan had one last gift. He handed Eden a bound book, its pages filled with the story of them.

Krista had taken the photos he collected, snapshots, selfies, and quiet moments he'd captured and crafted them into a keepsake that traced their days together, memories of their journey, page by page.

Eden looked at the book in her hands, the photos stirring every feeling she had kept close. A tear slipped down her cheek, a soft laugh followed, and warmth filled her chest. More than anything else, she knew she was in love with Donovan and grateful for the life they were building together.

Across the room, laughter rose again.

Krista's phone buzzed. Then Eden's.

The photo was live. The caption: *Jubilee*.

Eden surrounded by her people. Head thrown back mid-laugh. Donovan beside her, hand at her waist like it belonged there.

The internet did what it always does when it recognizes truth.

It responded.

The comments poured in.

One in particular, caught her attention.

It looks like love found you. Christopher's comment was a full circle moment, closing that loop.

Eden didn't reply. She lifted her glass instead.

"Happy birthday to me. Here's to fifty, let's do fifty more. To release. To return. To restoration."

Cheers echoed.

And as Donovan's hand tightened just slightly into hers, Eden understood with absolute certainty.

This wasn't the end of her story.

It was the beginning of a new one.

Epilogue

Six months after her fiftieth birthday, Eden sat at a table flooded with late-morning light. Across from her sat Donovan, Marcel, and Katy, papers spread between matcha lattes and laughter breaking out every few minutes.

They had built something together.

It didn't happen overnight, and it didn't happen by accident.

She twisted the new ring on her finger, still getting used to its weight and size.

What began as a modest idea was growing into a firm with a clear soul. A place where stories were honored. Where capital met consciousness, and where power was treated as stewardship instead of entitlement. They didn't announce themselves loudly. They didn't need to. The right people were finding them. And the Metropolitan Community Equity Alliance was their first client.

Their firm had successfully negotiated another multi-year project to revitalize a historic district, combining education, entrepreneurship, and the arts. Proof their impact was no longer abstract; it was tangible.

And Eden herself felt the pull of a new Jubilee, a plan to mentor young women in business and faith, helping them discover purpose and voice, just as she had.

The philanthropic storyteller gave them their own show on her network, trusting them to shape narratives that didn't just inform but transform.

Eden's gifts hadn't just made room for her; she was now creating the rooms that once tried to leave her out.

Krista and Daniel were considering moving back home, anchoring their lives where the work and the calling now lived.

And then there was the Jubilee Fund.

It unfolded naturally, doing exactly what Jubilee was always meant to do. Releasing what had been held too tightly. Returning what had been delayed. Restoring what once felt improbable. It funded political candidates who led with integrity. Supported neighborhood revitalization. Created gift card programs for older children often overlooked. Invested in community development with patience and care.

Eden often thought about the letter that started everything. The one that arrived before she was ready to receive it. It felt strange now to image a version of herself who hadn't trusted the time of who she would become.

She often whispered thanks to her godfather, Laurence.

She had truly walked into her everything season.

Donovan sat beside her like someone who assumed his rightful position. The love he offered did not interrupt her life. It expanded it.

Grant and Amara were planning a destination vow-renewal cere-
mony, and everyone is now making plans to attend.

The day after Eden's fiftieth birthday, on New Year's Eve, Marcel
proposed to Katy. She said yes immediately, laughing through tears.

By spring, wedding plans were underway.

By summer, they were married.

And by fall, there was news.

Life, it seemed, could be generous when it was trusted.

Eden and Donovan were asked to be godparents.

The symmetry didn't escape her. She would now stand where Laurence and Millie once stood, watching over a future not her own, but
entrusted to her care.

Little Miss Millicent Eden Rogers would be making her arrival in
the spring.

Time wasn't repeating itself. It was completing a cycle.

Katy leaned back in her chair one morning, appreciating the work
they'd built and the love that had taken root alongside it. She never
said, "I told you so," but the quiet smile she wore said enough. Her instincts had been right. Playing a little elf, a little cupid, had been worth
the risk. Not everything had gone according to plan, but enough of it
had. Love had shown up anyway.

On certain mornings, Eden still woke up early. She sat still in devotion before the world asked anything of her. She listened for the small
nudges.

She learned that love is meant to be lived and that Jubilee isn't tied
to an age or number necessarily but to a mindset.

And as Eden moved through her days now, she carried what it had
taken her fifty years to learn. She was never behind. Never overlooked.
Never late.

Her story, as it turns out, was just getting started.

9 Set apart the fiftieth year as holy, and proclaim liberty to everyone living in the land. This is your jubilee year. Every slave will be freed in order to return to his property and to his family. **11** That fiftieth year will be your jubilee year. Don't plant or harvest what grows by itself or pick grapes from the vines in the land. **12** The jubilee ☐year☐ will be holy to you. You will eat what the field itself produces.

Leviticus 25:9-12 (**GNT**)

About the Author

Shakira R. Thompson, a natural-born storyteller has submitted to her God-given talents and have allowed them to transform her into an author, publisher, and entrepreneur.

Born with the spark of romance in her heart, Shakira, has an unwavering passion for all things romance. She crafts heartwarming stories that feel real and true while transcending barriers. As the founder and visionary behind Love Story 365, she fearlessly leads a movement, putting love on full display in all its forms.

With unwavering faith in a guiding hand, she compellingly believes love is no mere coincidence – it is a divine masterpiece crafted with purpose and intention. These days, Shakira believes she is living her life according to Ephesians 2:10:

> *"For we are his workmanship, created in Christ Jesus unto good works, which God hath before ordained that we should walk in them." (KJV)*